"Still can't resist the sports guys?"

"I'm a slow learner."

She'd been anything but a slow learner the one time they'd had sex. She'd been the sweetest thing he'd ever tasted.

He cursed silently. He had to stop thinking about her. Even though right now the sunlight from a nearby window caught in her hair, creating a halo effect, and illuminated the fascinating flecks in her eyes. But what really drew him was the bow of her mouth. Soft, pink and unadorned—just waiting to be kissed, even now, fifteen years later.

She frowned. "Are you okay?"

"Fine. I'm stalked by schoolteachers all the time."

She flushed.

"If you came to get my attention, you've got it."

* * *

Second Chance with the CEO is part of the The Serenghetti Brothers series—In business and the bedroom, these alpha brothers drive a hard bargain!

Dear Reader,

It's good to be writing for Harlequin Desire again after taking time to attend to family! This is my thirteenth Desire book, and the first in a series about the Serenghetti family—four powerful, passionate Italian-American siblings!

Teacher Marisa Danieli needs a fantastic headliner for the Pershing School fund-raiser in order to earn a job promotion. Unfortunately, her best bet is sweet-talking Cole Serenghetti—former professional hockey player returned to the family fold as CEO of Serenghetti Construction, high school troublemaker and, most important, her disastrous teenage crush... until she got him suspended from school.

Cole would rather eat an ice puck than headline Marisa's fund-raiser, but fairly soon, thanks to one steamy kiss in a bar for the sake of their exes, everyone believes that Marisa and Cole are a couple. The second time around, will everything work out for Pershing's most scandalous fake couple, or will history repeat itself?

Watch out for more stories about the Serenghetti siblings, coming soon from Harlequin Desire!

Warmest wishes,

Anna

Website: www.annadepalo.com

Facebook: www.Facebook.com/AnnaDePaloBooks

Twitter: @Anna_DePalo

ANNA DePALO

SECOND CHANCE
WITH THE CEO

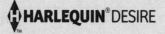

Recycling programs
for this product may
not exist in your area.

ISBN-13: 978-0-373-73485-6

Second Chance with the CEO

Copyright © 2016 by Anna DePalo

Printed in U.S.A.

www.Harlequin.com

USA TODAY bestselling author **Anna DePalo** is a Harvard graduate and former intellectual-property attorney who lives with her husband, son and daughter in her native New York. She writes sexy, humorous books that have been published in more than twenty countries and has won the RT Reviewers' Choice Award, the Golden Leaf and the Book Buyers Best Award. For the latest news, sign up for her newsletter at annadepalo.com.

Books by Anna DePalo

Harlequin Desire

Having the Tycoon's Baby
Under the Tycoon's Protection
Tycoon Takes Revenge
Cause for Scandal
Captivated by the Tycoon
An Improper Affair
Millionaire's Wedding Revenge
CEO's Marriage Seduction
The Billionaire in Penthouse B
His Black Sheep Bride
One Night with Prince Charming
Improperly Wed

The Serenghetti Brothers

Second Chance with the CEO

Visit her Author Profile page at Harlequin.com, or annadepalo.com, for more titles.

For Colby, Nicholas & Olivia,
for understanding that I write.

One

"Cole Serenghetti," she muttered, "come out, come out, wherever you are."

She knew she sounded like a corny fairy-tale character, but she'd been short on happy endings lately, and the words couldn't hurt, could they?

Then again, there was always *be careful what you wish for...*

As if she'd conjured him, a tall man appeared under a crossbeam at the construction site.

A feeling of dread curled in her stomach. How many times had she started out thinking she could do this and then her courage had flagged? Three? Four?

Still, the students at Pershing School depended on her bringing Cole Serenghetti to heel—her job could hinge on it, as well.

Marisa lifted her hand from the steering wheel and

squeezed it to stop a sudden tremor. Then she raised her field glasses.

Features obscured under his yellow hard hat, the man strode down the dirt path leading to the opening in the chain-link fence surrounding the construction site, which would soon be a four-story medical office complex. Clad in jeans, a plaid shirt and vest and work boots, he could have been just any other construction worker. But he had an air of command…and his physique showed potential for inclusion in a beefcake calendar.

Marisa's heart pounded hard in her chest.

Cole Serenghetti. Former professional hockey player returned to the family fold as CEO of Serenghetti Construction, high school troublemaker and her disastrous teenage crush.

Could the package be worse?

Marisa slunk lower in the driver's seat, letting the binoculars dangle against her chest from their cord. The last thing she needed was for a police officer to come around and ask why she was stalking a rich bad-boy real estate developer.

Blackmail? Pregnant with his child? Planning to steal his Range Rover, parked oh-so-tantalizingly close and unguarded at the curb of the office building under construction?

Would anyone believe that the truth was much more mundane? Everyone knew her as Miss Danieli, sweet-natured teacher at the Pershing School. Ironic if her new secret life as a millionaire stalker came at the cost of her job and reputation when all she was trying to do was help the high school-aged students at her college-preparatory school.

Tossing aside her field glasses, she popped out of her Ford Focus and darted down the street, her open coat flapping around her, as her quarry reached the sidewalk. There were no pedestrians on this side street at four in the afternoon, though it was nearing evening rush in the city of Springfield. She'd seen construction workers earlier, but there were none on the street now.

As she approached, the dank smells of the construction site hit her. It was dirty, and the air was heavy with particles that she could almost feel, even in the damp cold that clung to western Massachusetts in March.

She heard her stomach grumble. She'd been too nervous about this meeting to eat lunch.

"Cole Serenghetti?"

He turned his head while taking off his hard hat.

Marisa slowed her steps as she was jerked back in time by the sight of the dark, ruffled hair, the hazel eyes and the chiseled lips. A scar now bisected his left cheek, joining the small one on his chin that had been there in high school.

Marisa felt her heart squeeze. His newest scar looked as if it had hurt—*bad.*

But he was still the sexiest man she'd ever crossed.

She tried hard to hold on to her scattered thoughts even as she drank in the changes in him.

He was bigger and broader than he'd been at eighteen, and his face had more hard planes. But the charisma of being a former National Hockey League star—and sex symbol—turned millionaire developer was the biggest change of all. And while he sported the new scar, he showed no signs of the injury that had been serious enough to end his hockey career. He moved fine.

Even though Pershing was located on the outskirts

of Welsdale, Massachusetts, the town that the Serenghettis called home, she hadn't been anywhere near
Cole since high school.

She didn't miss the once-over he gave her, and then
a slow smile lit his face.

Relief swept through her. She'd been dreading this
reunion ever since high school, but he seemed willing
to put the past behind them.

"Sweetness, even if I wasn't Cole Serenghetti, I'd be
saying yes to you." The lazy smile stayed on his face
but his gaze traveled downward again, lingering on the
cleavage revealed by her long-sleeved dress, and then
on her legs, shown off by her favorite wedge-heeled
espadrilles.

Oh...crap.

Cole looked up and smiled into her eyes. "You're
a welcome ray of sunshine after a muddy construction site."

He didn't even recognize her. Crazy giddiness welled
up inside. She'd never forgotten him in the past fifteen
years, worrying over her betrayal—and his. And all
that time, he'd been sleeping like a baby.

She knew she looked different. Her hair was loose
for a change and highlighted, the ends shorter and curling around her shoulders. Her figure was fuller, and her
face was no longer hidden behind owlish glasses. But
still...she plummeted to Earth like a hang glider that
had lost the wind.

*She had to get this over with, much as she hated to
end the party.*

She took a steadying breath. "Marisa Danieli. How
are you, Cole?"

The moment hung between them, stretching out.

Then Cole's face closed, his smile dimming.

She curved her lips tentatively. "I'm hoping to hold you to that *yes*."

"Think again."

Ouch. Well, this was more like the script that had been playing in her head. She forced herself to keep up the polite professionalism without, she hoped, tipping into desperation. "It's been a long time."

"Not long enough." He assessed her. "And I'm guessing it's no accident you're here now—" he quirked a brow "—unless you've developed a weird compulsion to prowl construction sites?"

She'd always been bad at door-to-door solicitation jobs, and now, it seemed, was no exception. *Breathe. Breathe.* "The Pershing School needs your help. We're reaching out to our most important alumni."

"We?"

She nodded. "I teach tenth-grade English there."

Cole twisted his lips. "They're still putting their best foot forward."

"Their only foot. I'm the head of fund-raising."

He narrowed his eyes. "Congratulations and good luck."

He stepped around her, and she turned with him.

"If you'll just listen—"

"To your pitch?" He shot her a sideways look. "I'm not as big a sucker for the doe-eyed look as I was fifteen years ago."

She filed away *doe-eyed* for later examination. "Pershing needs a new gym. I'm sure that as a professional hockey player, you can appreciate—"

"*Former* NHL player. Check the yearbook for athletics. You'll come up with other names."

"Yours was at the top of the list." She picked her way over broken sidewalk, trying to keep up with his stride. Her espadrilles had seemed like a good choice for a school day. Now she wished she'd worn something else.

Cole stopped and swung toward her, causing her to nearly run into him. "Still at the top of your list?" He lifted his mouth in a sardonic smile. "I should be flattered."

Marisa felt the heat sting her cheeks. He made it sound as if she was throwing herself at him all over again—and he was rejecting her.

She had an abysmal record with men—wasn't her recent broken engagement further proof?—and her streak had started with Cole in high school. Humiliation burned like fire.

A long time ago she and Cole would have had their heads bent together over a book. She could have shifted in her seat and brushed his leg. In fact, she had brushed his leg, more than once, and he'd touched his lips to hers…

She plunged ahead. "Pershing needs your help. We need a headliner for our fund-raiser in a couple of months to raise money for the new gym."

He looked implacable, except that twin flames danced in his eyes. "You mean *you* need a headliner. Try your pitch on someone else."

"The fund-raiser would be good for Serenghetti Construction, too," she tried, having rehearsed her bullet points. "It's an excellent opportunity to further community relations."

He turned away again, and she placed a staying hand on his arm.

Immediately, she realized her mistake.

They both looked down at his biceps, and she yanked her hand back.

She'd felt him, strong and vital, his arm flexing. Once, fifteen years ago, she'd run her hands over his arms and moaned his name, and he'd taken her breast in his mouth. *Would she ever stop having a heated response to his every touch, every look and every word?*

She stared into his eyes, which were now hard and indecipherable—as tough as the rocks he blasted for a living.

"You need something from me," he stated flatly.

She nodded, her throat dry, feeling hot despite the weather.

"Too bad I don't forgive or forget a deliberate betrayal easily. Consider it a character flaw that I can't forget the facts."

She flushed. She'd always wondered whether he'd known for certain who'd ratted out his prank to the school administration, earning him a suspension and likely costing Pershing the hockey championship that year. Now it seemed she had her answer.

She'd had her reasons for doing what she'd done, but she doubted they'd have satisfied him—then or now.

"High school was a long time ago, Cole," she said, her voice thin.

"Right, and in the past is where the two of us are going to stay."

His words hurt even though it had been fifteen years. Her chest felt tight, and it was difficult to breathe.

He nodded at the curb. "Yours?"

She hadn't realized it, but they were near her car. "Yes."

He pulled open her door, and she stepped off the curb.

A swimming sensation came over her, and she swayed.

Still, she tried for a dignified exit. A few more steps and she'd put an end to this uncomfortable reunion…

As the edges of her vision faded to black, she had one last thought. *I should have eaten lunch.*

She heard Cole curse and his hard hat hit the ground. He caught her in his arms as she slumped against him.

When she floated to consciousness again, Cole was saying her name.

For a moment she thought she was fantasizing about their sexual encounter in high school…until the smells of the construction site penetrated her brain, and she realized what had happened.

She was cradled against a warm, solid body. Her trench coat was bunched around her like a cocoon.

She opened her eyes, and her gaze connected with Cole's. His golden-green eyes were intense.

She was also up close and personal with the new scar traversing his cheek. It looked painful but not jagged. *Had he taken a skate blade to the face?* She wanted to reach up and trace it.

He frowned. "Are you okay?"

Heat rushed to her cheeks. "Yes, let me down."

"May be a bad idea. Are you sure you can stand?"

Whatever the effects were of his career-ending injury, he seemed to have no problem holding a curvy woman of medium height in his arms. He was all hard muscle and restrained power.

"I'm fine! Really."

Looking as if he still had misgivings, Cole lowered his arm. When her feet hit the ground, he stepped back.

Her humiliation was complete. So total, she couldn't bear to face it right now.

"Just like old times," Cole remarked, his tone tinged with irony.

As if she needed the reminder. She'd fainted during one of their study sessions in high school. It was how she'd first wound up in his arms...

"How long was I out?" she asked, not meeting his eyes.

"Less than a minute." He shoved his hands in his pockets. "Are you all right?"

"Perfectly fine. I haven't been to an emergency room since I was a kid."

"You still have a tendency to faint."

She shook her head, looking anywhere but at him. *Talk about being overwhelmed by seeing him again.* Anticipating and yet dreading this meeting, she'd been too nervous to eat. "No, I haven't fainted in years. The medical term is vasovagal syncope, but my episodes are very infrequent."

Except she had a terrible habit of fainting around him. It was their first meeting in fifteen years, and she'd already managed a replay of high school. She didn't even want to consider what *he* was thinking right now. Probably that she was a consummate schemer with great acting skills.

He suddenly looked bland and aloof. "You couldn't have planned a better Hail Mary pass."

She cringed inwardly. He was suggesting that fainting had allowed her to buy time and get his sympathy. She was too embarrassed to get angry, however. "You play hockey, not football. Hail Mary is football. And why would I want to make a desperate last move with little chance of success?"

He shrugged his shoulders. "Confuse the other side."

"And did I?"

He looked as if he wished he were wearing all the protective gear of a hockey uniform. She was throwing *him* off balance. She was dizzy with momentary power, though her arms and legs still felt rubbery.

"I haven't changed my mind."

She lowered her shoulders and stepped toward her car.

"Are you okay to drive?" he asked, hands still shoved into his pockets.

"Yes. I feel fine now." *Tired, defeated and mortified, but fine.*

"Goodbye, Marisa."

He'd closed the door on her years ago, and now he was doing it again, with a note of finality in his voice.

She pushed aside the unexpectedly forceful emotional pain. As she stepped into her car, she was aware of Cole's brooding gaze on her. And when she pulled away, she glanced in her rearview mirror and saw that he was still watching her from the curb.

She should never have come. And yet, she had to get him to say yes. She hadn't come this far to accept defeat like this.

"You look like a man in need of a punching bag," Jordan Serenghetti remarked, hitting his boxing gloves together. "I'll spring for this round."

"Lucky bastard," Cole responded, moving his head from side to side, loosening up. "You get to work out the kinks by slamming someone on the ice rink."

Jordan still had a high-velocity NHL career with the New England Razors, whereas Cole's own had finished with a career-ending injury.

Still, whenever Jordan was in town, the two of them had a standing appointment in the boxing ring. For Cole, it beat the monotony of working out at the gym. Even as a construction executive, it paid to lead by example and stay in shape.

"Next hockey game isn't for another three days," Jordan responded, approaching with gloves raised. "That's a long time to be holding punches. Anyway, don't you have a babe to work out the kinks with?"

Marisa Danieli was a babe, all right, but Cole would be damned if he worked out anything with her. Unfortunately, she'd intruded on his thoughts too often since she'd dropped back into his arms last Friday.

Jordan touched a glove to his boxing helmet and then grinned. "Oh yeah, I forgot. Vicki dumped you for the sports agent—what's his name, again?"

"Sal Piazza," Cole said and sidestepped Jordan's first jab.

"Right, Salami Pizza."

Cole grunted. "Vicki didn't dump me. She—"

"Got tired of your inability to commit."

Cole hit Jordan with his right. "She wasn't looking for commitment. It was the perfect fling that way."

"Only because she'd heard of your reputation, so she knew she had to move on."

"As I said, everyone was happy." They danced around the ring, oblivious to the gym noises around them.

Even on a Wednesday evening, Jimmy's Boxing Gym was humming with activity. The facility was kept cold but even the cool air couldn't diminish the smell of sweat and sounds of exertion under the fluorescent lights.

Jordan rolled his neck. "You know, Mom wants you to settle down."

Cole bared his teeth. "She'd also be happy if you quit risking thousands of dollars in orthodontia on the ice rink, but that's not going to happen, either."

"She can pin her hopes on Rick, then," Jordan said, referring to their middle brother, "if anyone knew where he was."

"On a movie set on the Italian Riviera, I've heard."

Their brother was a stuntman, the risk taker among them, which was saying a lot. Their long-suffering mother claimed she'd lived at the emergency room while raising three boys and a girl. It was true they'd all broken bones, at one time or another, but Camilla Serenghetti still wasn't aware of her sons' most hair-raising thrills.

"It figures he's on a paparazzi-riddled set," Jordan grumbled. "No doubt there's at least one hot actress in the picture."

"Mom has Mia to fall back on, even if she is in New York." Their youngest sibling was off pursuing a career as a fashion designer, which meant Cole was the only one based in Welsdale full-time.

"It sucks being the oldest, Cole," Jordan said, as if reading his thoughts, "but you've got to admit you're more suited to run Serenghetti Construction than any of the rest of us."

In the aftermath of Cole's career-ending hockey injury, their father, Serg, had suffered a debilitating stroke. Cole had grasped the reins of Serenghetti Construction eight months ago and never let go.

"It doesn't suck," Cole said. "It just needs to be done."

He took the opportunity to hit Jordan with a surprise right. Damn, it felt good to rid himself of some frustration in the ring. He loved his brother, so it stunk to be even a little envious of Jordan's life. It wasn't just that Jordan was still a star with the Razors, because Cole had had a good run with the team himself. His younger brother also enjoyed a freedom missing from Cole's own life these days.

Their father had always hoped one or more of his sons would carry on the family business. And in the casino of life, Cole had drawn the winning card.

Cole had been familiar with the construction business ever since he'd spent summers working on sites as a teenager. He just hadn't anticipated having his hockey dream cut short and needing to pull his family together at the same time. Business had been tight until recently, and with Serg nearly flat on his back, Cole had been doing some scrambling with the hand he'd been dealt.

With any luck, one way or another, Cole could get on with his life again soon. Even if his future wasn't on the ice, he had his own business and investment opportunities to pursue, particularly in the sports field. Coaching, for one thing, was beckoning…

"So why don't you tell me what's got you in a bad mood?" Jordan asked, as if they weren't in a ring trying to knock each other off their feet.

Cole's mind went to his more immediate problem—if she could even be called that instead of…oh yeah, a wrecking ball in heels. He built things, and she destroyed them—dreams being at the top of her list. *Best remember her evil powers.* "Marisa Danieli stopped by the construction site today."

Jordan looked puzzled.

"High school," Cole elaborated and then watched his brother's frown disappear.

He and his brothers had graduated from different high schools, but Jordan knew of Marisa. After her pivotal role in Cole's suspension during senior year, she had for a time become infamous among the Serenghetti brothers and their crowd.

"Luscious Lola Danieli?" Jordan asked, the side of his mouth turning up.

Cole had never liked the nickname—and that was even before he'd started thinking of Marisa Lola Danieli as the high school Lolita who had led him down the path to destruction. She'd earned the tongue-in-cheek nickname in high school because she'd dressed and acted the opposite of sexy.

He hadn't told anyone about his intimate past with Marisa. His brothers would have had a field day with the story of The Geek and The Jock. As far as anyone knew, she was just the girl who'd scored off him—ratting out his prank to the principal like a hockey player slapping the puck into the goal for the game-winning shot.

For years the moment the principal had let slip that Marisa was the person who'd blabbed about him had been seared into his memory. He'd never pulled another prank again.

Still, he wasn't merely dwelling on what had happened when they'd been about to graduate. The fact that his hockey career had ended in the past year made it bad timing for Marisa to show up and remind him of how close she'd come to derailing it before it had begun. And as he'd told Jordan, he'd accepted his new role as CEO, but it wasn't without its frustrations. He was still on a big learning curve trying to drive Serenghetti Construction forward.

His brother's punch caught him full on the shoulder, sending him staggering. He brought his mind back to what was happening in the ring.

"Come on. Show me what you've got," Jordan jeered, warming up. "I haven't run into Marisa since you two graduated from Pershing."

"Until today, I could say the same thing," Cole replied.

"So, what? She's come back for round two now that you're on your feet again?"

"Hilarious."

"I was always the funny brother."

"Your sense of fraternal loyalty warms my heart," he mocked.

Jordan held up his hands in a gesture of surrender, nearly coming to a stop. "Hey, I'm not defending what she did. It sucked big-time for you to miss the final game and for Pershing to lose the hockey championship. Everyone avoided her wherever she went in town. But people can change."

Cole hit his brother with his left. "She wants me to headline a fund-raiser so Pershing can build a new gym."

Jordan grunted and then gave a low whistle. "Or maybe not. She's still got guts."

Marisa had changed, but Cole wasn't going to elaborate for his brother. These days there'd be nothing tongue-in-cheek about the nickname Luscious Lola, and that was the damn problem.

Before he'd recognized her, his senses had gone on high alert, and his libido had gleefully raced to catch up. The woman was sex in heels. It should be criminal for a schoolteacher to look like her.

The eyeglasses that she used to wear in high school were gone, and her hair was longer and loose—the ends curling in fat, bouncy curls against her shoulders. She was no longer hiding her figure under shapeless sweatshirts, and she'd filled out in all the right places. Everything was fuller, curvier and more womanly. He should know—once he'd run his hands over those breasts and thighs.

Before she'd announced who she was, he'd been thinking the gods of TGIF were smiling down at him at the end of a long workweek. Then he'd gotten a reprieve until she'd literally fallen into his arms—a one-two punch.

In those seconds staring down into her face, he'd been swamped by conflicting emotions: surprise, anger, concern and yeah, lust. More or less par for the course for him where Marisa was concerned. He could still feel the imprint of her soft curves. She sent signals that bypassed the thinking part of his brain and went straight to the place that wanted to mate.

Jordan caught him square on the chest this time. "Come on, come on. You're dazed. Woman on your mind?"

Cole lifted his lips in a humorless smile. "She suggested that participating in the fund-raiser for Pershing might be good PR for Serenghetti Construction."

Jordan paused before dancing back a step. "Marisa is a smart cookie. Can't fault her there."

Cole grumbled. Marisa's suggestion made some sense though he'd rather have his front teeth knocked out than admit it. He'd never liked publicity and couldn't have cared less about his image during his professional hockey days, to the everlasting despair of his agent. And since taking over the reins at Serenghetti Construction, he'd been focused on mastering the ropes to keep the business operating smoothly. Community relations had taken a backseat.

Marisa had a brain, all right—in contrast to many of the women who'd chased after him in his pro days. She'd literally been a book-hugger in high school. The jocks in the locker room hadn't even been able to rate her because it had been hard to do reconnaissance.

He'd eventually had the chance to discover the answer—she'd been a C-cup bra. But the knowledge had ultimately come at a steep price.

These days he'd bet the house that she had an A-plus body. She was primed to set men on their path to crashing and burning, just like old times.

Except this time, her next victim wouldn't be him.

Two

Squash racquet back of hall closet. I'll pick it up.

Marisa hit the button to turn off her cell phone. The message from Sal had come while she was out. She'd been so shaken by talking to Cole for the first time in fifteen years that she hadn't realized she had a text until after she'd gotten back to her apartment.

Annoyance rose up in her. As far as text messages went, it wasn't rude. But it hadn't come from just anybody. It had come from her former fiancé, who'd broken things off three months ago.

During their brief engagement, she'd been sliding into the role of the good little wife, picking up Sal's dry cleaning and making runs to the supermarket for him. From Sal's perspective, asking her to retrieve his squash racquet from her hall closet was unquestionably fair game. No doubt Sal had an appointment to meet a client at the gym, because even sports agents had to establish their athleticism—though Sal played squash only once in a blue moon when an invitation was issued.

She contemplated heaving the racquet out the window and onto the lawn, and then asking Sal to come find it.

Before she could overrule her scruples, she heard someone turn the lock in the front door. She frowned, nonplussed. *Hadn't she asked Sal to return his key...?*

She yanked the door open, and her cousin Serafina stumbled inside.

Marisa relaxed. "Oh, it's you."

"Of course it's me," Serafina retorted, straightening. "You gave me a key to the apartment, remember?"

"Right." She'd been so lost in thought, she'd momentarily assumed Sal had come back to retrieve the racquet, letting himself in with an extra copy of the key. *And he was uptight enough to do it. The rat.*

She was glad now she'd kept her condo even when her relationship with Sal had started getting serious enough that they'd contemplated moving in together. She'd bought the small two-bedroom five years ago, and at the time, it had been a major step toward independence and security.

She wondered where Cole called home these days. In all likelihood, a sprawling penthouse loft. She wouldn't be surprised if he lived in one of his own constructions.

One thing was for sure. He was still one of Welsdale's hottest tickets while she... Well, shapely was the most forgiving adjective for her curves. She was still a nobody, even if she had a name at the Pershing School these days.

"What's with you?" Serafina asked, taking off her cross-body handbag and letting it slide to the floor.

"I was thinking of a place to bury Sal's squash racquet," she responded and then waved a hand at the back of the apartment. "It's in the hall closet."

"Nice." Serafina smiled. "But with all the dogs in this complex, someone's bound to sniff out the cadaver real quick."

"He needs it back." She'd been hurt when she'd been dumped. But notwithstanding her irritation at Sal at the moment, these days she simply wanted to move on.

Serafina's lips twitched. "The racquet is an innocent bystander. It's not like you to misdirect anger, especially the vindictive kind."

After a moment Marisa sighed and lowered her shoulders. "You're right. I'll tell him that I'm leaving it on the table in the building foyer downstairs."

Ever since her debacle with Cole in high school, she'd been worried about being thought of as a bitch. She didn't need Cole Serenghetti; she needed a therapist.

"But tell the jerk what he can go do with it!" Serafina added.

She gave her cousin a halfhearted smile. Serafina was a little taller than she was, and her hair was a wavy dirty blond. She'd been spared the curly dark brown locks that were the bane of Marisa's existence. But they both had the amber eyes that were a family trait on their mothers' side, and their facial features bore a resemblance. Anyone looking at them might guess they were related, though they had different last names: Danieli and Perini.

While they were growing up, Marisa had treated Sera as a younger sister. She'd passed along books and toys, and shared advice and clothes. More recently, having had her cousin as a roommate for a few months, until Serafina found a job in her field and an apartment, had been a real lifesaver. Marisa appreciated the company. And with respect to men, her cousin took no prisoners. Marisa figured she could learn a lot there.

"Now for some good news," Serafina announced. "I'm moving out."

"That's great!" Marisa forced herself to sound perky.

"Well, not now, but after my trip to Seattle next week to visit Aunt Filo and Co."

"I didn't mean I'm glad you're leaving, I meant I'm happy for you." Three weeks ago her cousin had received the news that she'd landed a permanent position. Serafina had also gotten plane tickets to see Aunt Filomena and her cousins before starting her new job.

Serafina laughed. "Oh, Marisa, you're adorable! I know you're happy for me."

"Adorable ceases to exist after age thirty." She was thirty-three, single and holding on to sexy by a fraying thread. *And* she'd recently been dumped by her fiancé.

Of course, Cole had been all sunshine and come-here-honey…until he'd recognized who she was. Then he'd turned dark and stormy.

Serafina searched her face. "What?"

Marisa turned, heading down the hall toward the kitchen. "I asked Cole Serenghetti to do the Pershing Shines Bright fund-raiser for the school."

She hadn't died of mortification when she approached him for a favor after all these years, but she'd come close. She'd fainted in his arms. A hot wave of embarrassment washed over her, stinging her face. *When would the humiliation end?*

Some decadent chocolate cake was in order right now. There should be some left in the fridge. A pity party was always better with dessert.

"And?" Serafina followed behind.

Marisa waved her hand. "It was like I always dreamt it would be. He jumped right on my proposal. Chills and thrills all around."

"Great…?"

"Lovely." She spied the cake container on her old scarred moveable island. "And yummy."

Cole Serenghetti qualified as yummy, too. There were probably women lined up to treat him as dessert. A decade and a half later he was looking better than ever. She'd seen the occasional picture of him in the press during his hockey days, but nothing was like experiencing the man in person.

And tangling with him was just as much a turn-yourself-inside-out experience as it had always been.

"Um, Marisa?"

Marisa set the cake container on the table. "Time for dessert, I think."

The kind in front of her, not the Cole Serenghetti variety, even though he probably thought of her as a man-eater.

Marisa uncovered the chocolate seven-layer cake. She'd been so insecure about her body around Sal— she had too many rounded curves to ever be considered svelte. But now that he was in the past, she felt free to indulge again. Of course, Sal had a new and skinny girlfriend. He'd found the person he was looking for, and she was the size of a runway model.

"So Cole was thrilled to see you?" Serafina probed.

"Ecstatic."

"Now I know you're being sarcastic."

Long after high school Marisa had told Sera about her past with Cole, and how things had heated up between her and the oldest Serenghetti brother during senior year—before they'd gone into a deep freeze. Her cousin knew Marisa had confessed that Cole was responsible for the ultimate school prank, that Cole had been suspended as a result and that Pershing had lost the Independent School League hockey championship soon after.

Getting out two plates and cutlery, Marisa said, "It's not a party unless you join me."

Serafina sat down in one of the kitchen chairs. "I hope this guy is worth five hundred calories. Let me guess, he still blames you for what you did in high school?"

"Bingo."

Marisa relayed snatches of her encounter with Cole, the way she'd been doing in her mind since leaving the construction site earlier. All the while, Cole's words reverberated in her head. *I'm not as big a sucker for the doe-eyed look as I was fifteen years ago.* Oh yes, he still held a grudge. He'd been impossible to sway about the fund-raiser. And yet, damningly, she felt a little frisson of excitement that he had fallen under the spell of her big, brown eyes long ago…

Serafina shook her head. "Men never grow up."

Marisa slid a piece of cake in front of her cousin. "It's complicated."

"Isn't it always? Cut yourself a bigger piece."

"All the cake in the world might not be enough."

"That bad, huh?"

Marisa met her cousin's gaze and nodded. Then she

took a bite of cake and got up again. "We need milk and coffee."

A little caffeine would help. She felt so tired in the aftermath of a faint.

She loaded water and coffee grinds into the pot and then plugged the thing into the outlet. She wished she could afford one of those fancy coffeemakers that were popular now, but they weren't in her budget.

Why had she ever agreed to approach Cole Serenghetti? She knew why. She was ambitious enough to want to be assistant principal. It was part of her long climb out of poverty. She credited her academic scholarship to Pershing with helping to turn her life around. And now that she was single and unattached again, she needed something to focus on. Pershing and her teaching job were the thing. *And* she owed it to the kids.

Marisa shook her head. She'd volunteered to be head of fund-raising at Pershing, but she hadn't anticipated that the current principal would be so set on getting Cole Serenghetti for their big event. She should have tried harder to talk Mr. Dobson out of it. But he'd discovered from the school yearbook that Cole and Marisa had been in the same graduating class, so he'd assumed Marisa could make a personal appeal to the hockey star, one former classmate to another. There was no way Marisa was going to explain how her high school romance with Cole had ended disastrously.

"So what are you going to do now?" Serafina asked as Marisa set two coffee mugs on the table.

"I don't know."

"It's not like you to give up so easily."

"You know me well."

"I've known you forever!"

Marisa summoned the determination that had helped her when she'd been the child of a single mother who worked two jobs. "I'll have to give it another try. I can't go back to the board admitting defeat this fast. But I can't lie in wait for Cole again at a construction site, like some crazed stalker."

Serafina wiped her mouth with a napkin. "You may want to give Jimmy's Boxing Gym a go."

"What?"

Serafina gave her an arch look. "It's beefcake central. Also, Cole Serenghetti is known to be a regular."

Marisa's brow puckered. "And you know this, how?"

"The guys down at the Puck & Shoot. The hockey players are regulars." Sera paused and pulled a face. "Jordan Serenghetti stops in from time to time."

Judging from Sera's expression, Marisa concluded her cousin didn't much care for the youngest Serenghetti brother.

"Are you doing more than moonlighting as a waitress there?" Marisa asked with mock severity.

Serafina shrugged. "If you hung out in bars, you wouldn't need the tip." Then she flashed a mischievous grin. "Use it in good health."

Of course Cole Serenghetti would go to a boxing gym. The place was most likely the diametric opposite of the fancy fitness center where Sal played squash. She'd given up her own membership—with guilty relief—when Sal had unsubscribed from their relationship.

She rolled her eyes heavenward. "What do I wear to a boxing gym…?"

"My guess is, the less, the better." Serafina curved her lips. "Everyone will be sweaty and hot, hot, hot…"

One week later...

Cole saw his chance in Jordan's sudden loss of focus and hit him hard, following up with a one-two punch that sent his brother staggering.

Then he paused and wiped his brow while he let Jordan regain his balance, because their purpose was to get some exercise and not to go for a knockout. "I don't want to ruin your pretty face. I'll save that thrill for the guys on the ice."

Jordan grimaced. "Thanks. One of us hasn't had his nose broken yet, and—" he focused over Cole's shoulder "—I need to talk pretty right now."

"What the hell?"

Jordan indicated the doorway with his chin.

When Cole turned around, he cursed.

Marisa was here, and from all the signs, she didn't have any more sense about a boxing gym than she did about showing up at a construction site in heels. She was drawing plenty of attention from the male clientele—and some were going back for a second look. But her gaze settled nowhere as she made her way toward the ring that he and Jordan were using. She looked pure and unaware of her sexuality in a floaty polka-dot dress that skimmed her curves. The heels and bouncy hair were back, too.

She was the perfect picture of an innocent little schoolteacher—except Cole knew better. Still, for all outward appearances, the tableau was Bambi surrounded by wolves.

"Now that," Jordan said from behind him, "is a welcome Wednesday night surprise."

Cole scowled. *Not for him, it wasn't.* He moved toward the ropes, pulling at the lacing of one glove with the other. A staff member for the gym came up to the side of the ring to help him.

"Where are you going?" Jordan called.

"Take a breather!"

"I saw her first," his brother joked, coming up alongside him.

From when they'd hit puberty, the Serenghetti brothers had one rule: whoever saw a woman first got to make a move.

Cole leveled his brother with a withering look as the gym assistant pulled off his gloves. "That is Marisa Danieli."

Jordan's eyes widened, and then a slow grin spread across his face. "Wow, she's changed."

"Not as much as you think. Hands off."

"Hey, I'm not the one who needs a warning. Who yanked off his gloves?" Jordan looked over Cole's shoulder and then raised his eyebrows.

Cole turned. Marisa had pulled the ropes apart and was stepping into the ring, one shapely leg after the other.

"This should be good," Jordan murmured.

"Shut up."

Cole pulled off his padded helmet. The front of his sleeveless shirt was damp with perspiration, and his sweatpants hung low on his hips. It was a far cry from the way he looked in meetings these days—where he often wore a jacket and tie.

He handed off his helmet before turning toward the woman who'd crept into his thoughts too often during the past week. Sweeping aside any need for pleasantries, he demanded, "How did you find me?"

Marisa hesitated, looking as if her bravado was leaving her now that she was facing her opponent in the ring. "A tip at the Puck & Shoot."

Cole figured he shouldn't be surprised she was a patron of the New England Razors' hangout. She could scout for her next victim at a sports bar, and it would be easy pickings.

Marisa took a deep breath, and Cole watched her chest rise and fall.

She smiled, but it didn't reach her eyes. "Let's start again. And how are you, too, Cole?"

"Is that how you start the day in school? Correcting your students' manners?"

"Sometimes," she admitted.

Jordan stepped forward. "Don't mind Cole. Mom sent us to Miss Daisy's School for Manners, but only one of us graduated." Jordan flashed the mega-kilowatt grin that had earned him an underwear advertising campaign. "I'm Jordan Serenghetti, Cole's brother. I'd shake your hand but as you can see—" he held up his gloves, his smile turning rueful "—I've been pounding Cole to a pulp."

Marisa blinked, her gaze moving from Jordan to Cole. "He doesn't look the worse for wear."

Cole's muscles tightened and bunched, and then he frowned. He should be used to compliments… Besides, he knew she had an ulterior motive—she still needed him for her fund-raiser.

"We stay away from faces," Jordan added, "but his nose has been broken and mine hasn't."

"Yes," she said, "I see…"

Cole knew what he looked like. Not bad, but not model-handsome like Jordan. He and his brother shared the same dark hair and tall build, but Jordan's eyes were green while his were hazel. And he'd always been more rough-hewn—not that it mattered at the moment.

Jordan flashed another smile at Marisa. "You may remember me from Cole's high school days."

Cole forced himself to remember the expensive orthodontia as the urge hit to rearrange his brother's teeth. He noticed how Jordan didn't reference the high school fiasco in which Marisa had had a starring role.

"Jordan Serenghetti… I know you from the sports news," Marisa said, sidestepping the whole sticky issue of high school.

Cole had had enough.

"You don't take no for an answer," Cole interrupted, and had the pleasure of seeing Marisa flush.

She turned her big doe eyes on him. "I'm hoping you'll reconsider, if you'll just listen to what I have to say."

"If he won't listen, I will," Jordan joked. "In fact, why don't we make an evening of it? Everything goes down better with a little champagne—unless you prefer wine?"

Cole gave his brother a hard stare, but Jordan kept his gaze on Marisa.

"The Pershing School needs a headliner for its Pershing Shines Bright benefit," Marisa said to Jordan.

"I'll do it," Jordan said.

"You didn't graduate from the Pershing School."

"A minor detail. I was a student for a while."

Marisa took a step and swayed, her heels failing to find firm ground in the ring. Cole reached out to steady her, but she grasped one of the ropes for support, and he let his arm fall back to his side.

Careful. Touching Marisa was a bad idea, as he'd been reminded only last week.

"Cole's the better choice because he graduated from Pershing," Marisa said, looking into his eyes. "I know you have some loyalty to your school. You had a few good hockey seasons there."

"And thanks to you, no championship."

She looked abashed and then recovered. "That has to do with me, not Pershing, and anyway, there's a new school principal."

"But you're the messenger."

"A very pretty one," Jordan volunteered.

Cole froze his brother with a look. He and Marisa had known each other in a carnal sense, which should make her off-limits to Jordan. But he wasn't about to let his brother in on those intimate details—which meant he was in a bind about issuing a warning. Jordan was a player who liked women, making Marisa a perfect target for the charm that he never seemed to turn off.

Jordan shrugged his shoulders. "Maybe it wasn't Marisa's fault."

None of them needed him to elaborate.

"It was me at the principal's office," she admitted.

"But you're sorry…?" Jordan prompted, throwing her a lifeline.

"I regret my role, yes," she said, looking pained.

Cole lowered his shoulders. He'd gotten the closest thing to an apology.

Still, Marisa had another motive for showing up today. And while he may have gotten over high school and his suspension a long time ago, forgiving and forgetting *her* treachery was still a long time coming…

Jordan shot him a speaking glance. "And Cole apologizes for being Cole."

Cole scowled. "Like hell."

They hadn't even touched on intimate levels of betrayal that Jordan knew nothing about.

Jordan gestured with his glove. "Okay, I typically leave the mediation talks to the NHL honchos, but let's give this one more try. Cole regrets messing up with his last prank."

"Right," Cole said tightly but then couldn't resist taking a shot at his brother to dislodge the satisfied look on his face. "Jordan, talk show host is not in your future."

His brother produced a wounded look. "Not even sportscaster?"

"Since we're all coming clean," Cole continued pleasantly, looking at Marisa, "why don't you tell me what's in this for you?"

She blinked. "I told you. I want to help the Pershing School get a new gym."

"No, how does this all help you personally?"

Marisa bit her lip. "Well… I hope I'll be considered for assistant principal someday."

"Now we're getting warmer," he said with satisfaction, cocking his head because this was the Marisa he expected—full of guile and hidden motives. "Funny, I had you pegged for the type who'd be walking up the aisle in a white dress by now and then juggling babies and teaching."

Marisa paled, and Cole's hand curled. She looked as if he'd scored a dead hit.

"I was engaged until a few months ago," she said in a low voice.

"Oh yeah? Anyone I know?" Had Marisa entrapped someone else from high school? Unlikely.

"Maybe. He's a sports agent named Sal Piazza."

Beside them, his brother whistled before Cole could react.

"You might know him," Marisa continued, "because he's now dating your last girlfriend. Or at least you were photographed in the stands at a hockey game with her. Vicki Salazar."

Damn.

"Hey, can this be called *entangled by proxy*?" Jordan interjected, his brow furrowing. "Or how about *engaged by one degree of separation*? Is that an oxymoron?"

Cole felt a muscle in his face working. His brother didn't know the half of it. "Put a lid on it, Jordan."

Cole looked around. They were attracting an audience. The speculative ones were wondering whether this was a lovers' spat and Marisa was his girlfriend—and whether they could intercept her as she made her way out of the gym. "This is ridiculous. The ring isn't the place for this conversation. We're a damn spectacle."

Marisa looked startled.

He fastened his hand on her arm against his better judgment. "Come on." He lifted the rope. "After you."

Marisa cast a glance at Jordan.

"He isn't coming," Cole said shortly.

Marisa stepped between the ropes and Cole followed, taking the wooden steps down to the gym floor.

Ignoring curious looks, he steered Marisa toward the back entrance—the one leading to the parking lot. When they reached the rear door, he turned to face her and said, "So you're engaged to Sal Piazza."

"I was." She lifted her chin. "Not anymore."

"Still can't resist the sports guys?"

"I'm a slow learner."

She'd been anything but a slow learner the one time they'd had sex. She'd been the sweetest thing he'd ever tasted.

He cursed silently. He had to stop thinking about her. Even though right now, the sunlight from a nearby window caught in her hair, creating a halo effect, and illuminated the fascinating flecks in her eyes. But what really drew him was the bow of her mouth. Soft, pink and unadorned—just waiting to be kissed, even now, fifteen years later.

She frowned. "Are you okay?"

"Fine. I'm stalked by schoolteachers all the time."

She flushed.

"If you came to get my attention, you've got it." He jerked his head toward the way they had come. "Along with that of most of the guys in there."

"It's not my problem if they have a fetish for overworked and underpaid educators."

He almost burst out laughing. "Your job of recruiting me makes you overworked and underpaid?"

She pursed her lips.

"Your sports agent fiancé didn't give you any pointers about recruiting athletes?" The dig rolled off his tongue, and then he cocked his head. "Funny, you don't strike me as Sal Piazza's type."

"I'm not." She smiled tightly, looking as if she'd be dangerous with a hockey stick right now. "He left me for Vicki."

"He cheated on you?"

"He denied it had gone as far as…sex. But he said he'd met someone else…and he was attracted to her."

Marisa looked as if she couldn't believe what she was telling him.

"So Sal Piazza broke up with you to get Vicki in bed." Cole smiled humorlessly. "I should warn the guy that Vicki prefers anything to a bed."

"Don't be crude."

Hell if he could puzzle out Sal. Vicki and Marisa couldn't even be compared. One was a zero-calorie diet cola—you could guzzle twenty and they wouldn't fill you up—and the other a decadent dessert that could kill you.

He was also still wrapping his head around the fact that Sal and Marisa had been engaged. Sal was a sports nut, center-court wannabe. And in high school at least, Marisa couldn't have cared less about sports— her hookup with the captain of the hockey team aside.

On the other hand, from the few times Cole had run into Sal at some sports-related event or another, he'd struck Cole as an affable, conventional kind of guy. Medium build, average looks—bland and colorless. No surprise if Marisa had thought of him as safe and reli- able. Not that the relationship with Sal had worked out the way she'd expected.

"When did the breakup happen?" he asked.

"In January."

Cole and Vicki had last seen each other in November.

"Worried that Vicki might have cheated on you with a mere sports agent?" Marisa asked archly.

"No." His involvement with Vicki had been so ca- sual it had barely qualified as a relationship. Still, he couldn't resist getting another reaction out of Marisa. "Even ex-hockey players rank above sports agents in the pecking order."

She got a spark in her eyes. "So, according to you, I've been on a downward trajectory since high school?"

"Only you can speak to that, sweet pea."

He felt some satisfaction at provoking her. She'd been working hard to maintain a crumbling wall of polite and professional civility between them.

"Your hubris leaves me breathless."

He smiled mirthlessly. "That's the effect that I often have on women, but it's because of my huge—"

"Stop!"

"—reputation. What did you think I was going to say?"

"You're impossible."

"So you give up?" He glanced around them. "Good match. We both got in some nice jabs. I accept your concession."

"The way you accepted my apology?"

He jerked his head toward the interior of the gym. "Is that what it was?"

She nodded. "Take it or leave it."

"And if I leave it?"

She twitched her lips, her eyes flashing. "Time to go for Plan B. Fortunately, Jordan's already given me one. Now all I need to do is convince the school that he'd be a good substitute."

She started to turn away, and Cole reached out and caught hold of her upper arm.

"Stay away from Jordan," he said. "You've already messed up one Serenghetti. Don't go for another."

He'd gotten first dibs on Marisa more than a decade ago. And given their history, first dibs held even now, whether Jordan knew the details or not.

"I'm flattered you think so highly of my evil powers, but Jordan is a big boy who can take care of himself."

"I'm not kidding."

"Neither am I. I'm running out of time to find a head-liner for the Pershing fund-raiser."

"Not Jordan."

She pulled out of his grasp. "We'll see. Goodbye, Cole."

Broodingly, Cole watched her exit the gym.

Their meeting hadn't ended the way she'd wanted, but it wasn't the way he'd envisioned it, either.

Damn it.

He had to keep her away from Jordan, and his script didn't include admitting, *I slept with her*.

Three

Cole had to wait a week to corner his brother because Jordan had three away games. But he figured their parents' house was as good a location as any for a showdown. As he exited his Range Rover, he looked up at the storm clouds. *Yup.* The weather fit his mood.

When he didn't spot Jordan's car on his parents' circular drive, he quelled his impatience. His brother would be here soon enough. Jordan had replied to his text and agreed they would both stop by the house this evening to check on how their parents were doing. So Cole would soon have blessed relief from the irritation that had been dogging him for the past week. Marisa and his brother—*over his cold dead body.*

Cole made his way to the front doors. The Serenghetti house was a Mediterranean villa with a red-tile roof and white walls. In warmer months, a lush garden was his mother's pride and joy, keeping both her and a landscaper busy. As Serg's construction business had grown, Cole's parents had traded up to bigger homes. The move to the Mediterranean villa had been completed when Cole was in middle school. Serg had built a house big enough to accommodate the Serenghetti brood as well as the occasional visiting relatives.

Cole's jaw tightened. If Jordan had been contacted by Marisa, then his brother needed to be warned off. His brother had to understand that Marisa couldn't be trusted. She may have changed since high school, but Cole wasn't taking any chances. On the other hand, if Marisa had been bluffing about asking Jordan to be her second choice, so much the better. Either way, Cole was going to make damn sure there wasn't anything going on.

Memories had snuck up on him ever since Marisa had traipsed back into his life. Yeah, he'd taken a lot for granted when he'd been at Pershing—his status as top jock, his popularity with girls and the financial security that allowed him a ride at a private school. Still, there'd been pressure. Pressure to perform. Pressure to *outperform himself*—on and off the ice. He'd set himself up for a fall by trying to outdo his biggest game, his latest prank, his most recent sexual experience…

Back in high school, Marisa had been outside his inner circle but had seemingly been able to look in without judging. At least that was what he'd thought. And then she'd betrayed him.

Sure, he hadn't liked it one bit when Jordan had turned his charm on Marisa at the boxing gym. But it was because he hated to see his brother make the same mistake he'd made. It had nothing to do with being territorial about a teenage fling. He didn't do jealousy. Marisa was an attractive woman, but he was old enough to know the pitfalls of acting on pure lust.

As a professional hockey player, he'd always had easy access to women. But after a while it had started to lose meaning. When Jordan had joined the NHL, he'd given his younger brother *the talk* about the temptations facing professional athletes from money and fame. Of course, Jordan was a seasoned pro these days—but Marisa presented a brand of secret and stealthy allure.

He should know.

Cole tensed as he recalled how ready Jordan had been to succumb to temptation last week. Because his brother had been on the road for away games since then, with any luck he'd been too busy for Marisa to reach him.

Cole opened the unlocked front door and let himself in. The sounds of "We Open in Venice" hit him, and he wondered if his mother was again playing all the songs from Cole Porter's *Kiss Me, Kate*. She loved the musical so much, she had named her firstborn after its legendary composer.

Cole thought his life didn't need a soundtrack—least of all, that of the musical based on Shakespeare's *Taming of the Shrew*. Still, was it a coincidence—or the universe sending him a message? He had about as much chance of taming Marisa as of returning to his professional hockey career right now. Not that he was going to try. He was only going to make sure that he and any other Serenghetti were outside Marisa's ambit.

He made his way to the back of the house, where he found his mother in the oversize kitchen. As usual, the house smelled of flowers, mouthwatering food aromas…and familial obligation.

"Cole," Camilla said, pronouncing the *e* at the end of his name like a short vowel. "A lovely surprise, *caro*."

Although his mother had learned English at a young age, she still had an accent and sprinkled her English with Italian. She'd met and married Serg when he'd been vacationing in Tuscany, and she'd been a twenty-one-year-old hotel front-desk employee. Before Serg had checked out in order to visit extended family in the hockey-mad region north of Venice, the two had struck up a romance.

"Hi, Mom." Cole snagged a fried zucchini from a bowl on the marble-topped kitchen island. "Where's Dad?"

"Resting." She waved a hand. "You know all these visitors make him tired. Today the home-care worker, the nurse and the physical therapy came."

"You mean the physical therapist?"

"I say that, no?"

Cole let it slide. His mother had a late-blossoming career as the host of a local cooking show. Viewers who wrote in liked her accent, and television executives believed it added the spice of authenticity to her show. For Cole, it was just another colorful aspect of his lovable but quirky family.

"You beat me to the food. Did you taste the gnocchi yet?"

Cole turned to see Jordan saunter into the kitchen. Cole figured his brother must have driven up as soon as he'd entered the house. "How do you know she prepared gnocchi?"

Jordan shrugged. "I texted Mom earlier. She's perfecting a recipe for next week's show, and we're the guinea pigs. Gnocchi with prosciutto, escarole and tomato."

Camilla brightened. "I tell you? The name of the show is goin' to change to *Flavors of Italy with Camilla Serenghetti*."

"That's great!" Jordan leaned in to give his mother a quick peck on the cheek.

Cole nodded. "Congratulations, Mom. You'll be challenging Lidia Bastianich in no time."

Camilla beamed. "My name in the *titolo*. Good, no?"

"Excellent," Cole said.

Camilla frowned. "But I need to schedule more guests."

"Isn't that the job of the program booker at the station?"

"It's my show."

Jordan made a warding-off gesture with his hands. "Remember when you had me on last year, Mom? I made you burn the onions that you were sautéing. And Cole here wasn't much better when he was a guest."

From Cole's perspective, he and Jordan had been worth something in the sex appeal department, but his mother's show would never have mass crossover appeal to the beer-and-chips sports crowd.

Before he could offer to sacrifice himself again on the altar of his mother's show-business career, Camilla started toward the fridge and said, "I need somebody new."

"I'll put in a word with the Razors," Jordan offered. "Marc Bellitti likes to cook. And maybe a member of the team can suggest someone with better skills in the kitchen than on the ice."

Cole turned to his brother. "Speaking of ice, great game for you last night. You would have scored another goal if Peltier hadn't body-checked you at the last second."

Jordan grumbled. "He's been a pain in the rear all season." Then keeping an eye on their mother, as if to make sure he wouldn't be overheard, he added, "Guy needs to get laid."

At the mention of sex, Cole locked his jaw. "Has Marisa Danieli contacted you?"

Jordan cast him an assessing look. "Why do you ask?"

"She still needs a guinea pig for her fund-raiser. As I understand it, you're eager guinea pig material."

Jordan's lips quirked. "Being the test subject isn't half bad sometimes. Anyway, she wanted you."

"I told her no."

"Admirable fortitude. The guys in the locker room would be impressed."

"I'm asking you to tell her no."

"It hasn't come up."

Cole relaxed his shoulders. "She hasn't tried to reach you?"

"Nope. And quit focusing on the decoy. I'm a bad one. There's something else you'll find a lot more interesting."

Camilla set a big bowl of gnocchi on the counter and announced, "I'm goin' to check on your father and be right back."

"Take your time, Mom." Cole knew his mother was worried about his father's rough road to recovery. It had been several months since the stroke, and Serg still had not made a complete recovery—if he ever would.

When their mother left, Cole turned to Jordan and wasted no time in getting to the point. "What is it?"

"Word is that the job for the new gym at the Pershing School is going to JM Construction."

Cole's lips thinned. *She'd done worse than get Jordan on board for her fund-raiser.*

As far as jobs went for a midsize construction company like Serenghetti or JM, the new gym at the Pershing School was small-fry. However, JM would get the attendant publicity and goodwill.

Damn it. They'd been outbid twice in the past few months by JM Construction. Like Serenghetti, JM operated in the New England region, though both sometimes took jobs farther afield. Serenghetti's main offices were in Welsdale—at Serg's insistence—but they kept a business suite in Boston for convenience, as well as a small satellite staff in Portland, Maine.

"You know this how?" Cole demanded of his brother.

"Guys talking down at the Puck & Shoot. If you hung out there, you'd know, too. You should try it."

"A lot happens at the Puck & Shoot." Cole recalled that Marisa had found out how to run him to ground from a tip at the bar.

"The drinks aren't bad, and the female clientele is even better."

"I'm surprised you haven't spotted Marisa there."

Jordan snagged a cold gnocchi from the bowl and popped it into his mouth. "She doesn't look like the type to be a sports bar regular."

"A lot about her may surprise you."

His brother swallowed and grinned. "I'm sure."

"Jordan."

"Anyway, I was killing time. Someone brought up

my recent ad campaign, so I mentioned an opportunity to do a little local promo for the Pershing School. I asked if anyone was interested."

"Putting in a good word for Marisa?" Cole asked sardonically.

There was laughter in Jordan's eyes. "Well, I knew you didn't want to volunteer. And you'd have my head on a platter if I did the fund-raiser."

"Good call."

"But I felt bad for her, to be honest. She was even willing to tangle with you in order to find a celebrity."

"She knows what she's doing."

"She seems like a good sort these days. Or at least her cause is a good one."

"Right." *Whose side was his brother on?*

"Anyway, you remember Jenkins? He graduated a couple of years after you did and played in the minors for a while?"

"Yeah?"

"He said the rumor was that JM Construction had the inside track on building the gym. So he thought it was curious I was mentioning the school fund-raiser to the Razors. He indicated it was mighty magnanimous of me to try to find a recruit for JM's cause."

"Oh yeah, it was." Cole resisted a snort. "Still feeling sorry for Marisa?"

The woman had more up her sleeve than a cardsharp.

Jordan shrugged. "She may know nothing about who's getting the construction contract."

"We'll see. Either way, I'm about to find out."

Life was full of firsts—some of them more welcome than others. Cole had been her earliest lover, and now he was giving her another first. Marisa stepped inside Serenghetti Construction's offices, which she'd never done before.

The company occupied the uppermost floors of a redbrick building that had once been a factory, square in the middle of Welsdale's downtown. The website stated that Serg Serenghetti had renovated the building twenty years ago and turned it into a modern office complex. For years she'd felt as if she would never be welcome inside, but now she'd gotten a personal invite from Cole Serenghetti himself. It showed how life could turn on a dime.

Of course the actual call had come from Cole's assistant. But Marisa had taken it as a sign that Cole might be softening his stance. She was willing to hold on to any thread of hope, no matter how thin. Because as much as she'd bluffed, she had no Plan B. She hadn't tried to contact Jordan Serenghetti because it would be preferable for Pershing to have someone who'd graduated from the school as a headliner. Besides, she was sure Cole would block any attempt to recruit his brother.

In the lobby, Marisa tried not to be intimidated by the sleek glass-and-chrome design—a testament to money and power. And when she reached the top floor, she took a deep breath as she entered Serenghetti's spacious and airy offices. The decor was muted beiges and grays—cool and professional. The receptionist announced her, took her coat and then directed her down the hall to a corner office.

Her heart beat in a staccato rhythm as she reached an open doorway. And then her gaze connected with Cole's. He was standing beside an imposing L-shaped desk.

The air hummed between them, and Marisa steadied herself as she walked forward into his office. She'd dressed professionally in a beige pantsuit, but she was suddenly very aware of her femininity. That was because Cole exuded power in a navy suit and patterned tie. This was a different incarnation than his hockey uniform, or his hardhat and jeans, but no less potent.

"You look wary," Cole said. "Afraid you're in for a third strike?"

"You don't play baseball."

"Lucky you."

"You wouldn't have summoned me if you'd meant to turn me down again."

"Or maybe I'm a sadistic bastard who enjoys making you pay for past transgressions again and again."

Marisa compressed her lips to keep from giving her opinion. His office was devoid of personal items like family photos and as inscrutable as the man himself. She wondered if this room had been Serg's office until recently, or whether Cole had just avoided settling in by bringing mementos.

Cole smiled but it didn't reach his eyes. "So here's the deal, sweet pea. Serenghetti Construction builds the new gym at Pershing, no questions asked. I don't want to hear any garbage about handing off the job to a friend of a board member."

"What?"

"Yeah, surprised?" he asked as he prowled toward her. "So am I. I've been almost dancing with shock ever since I discovered you wanted me to be a poster boy for someone else's construction job. And not just anyone else, but our main competitor. They've underbid us on the last two jobs. But that's quality for you."

"I'm sure the construction would be up to code. We'd have an inspection," she said crossly.

"Being up to code is the least of your worries."

Marisa felt as if she'd shown up in the middle of the second act of a play. There was a context that she was missing here. "I have no idea what you're talking about. What friend of a board member?"

Cole scanned her face for a moment, then two. "It would figure they didn't let the teacher in on the discussion. Have you ever sat on a board of directors?"

She shook her head.

"The meetings might be public, but there's plenty of wheeling and dealing behind the scenes. It's you scratch my back, I'll scratch yours. We'll go with the headliner you want for the fund-raiser, but you'll back my guy for the construction job."

Marisa felt the heat of embarrassment flood her face. She'd thought she'd been so clever in her approach for Pershing Shines Bright. She hadn't even let Mr. Dobson know she'd talked to Cole because she'd thought her chances of success were uncertain at best. She'd wanted the option of persuading Mr. Dobson to go with someone else without the appearance that she'd failed.

Now she felt like a nitwit—one who didn't know what the other hand was doing. Or at least, didn't know what the school board was up to. She wanted to slump into a chair, but it would give Cole an even bigger advantage than he had.

"That kind of horse-trading is corrupt," she managed.

"That's life."

"I didn't have any idea."

"Right."

"You believe me?"

He made an impatient sound. "You're a walking, breathing cliché. In this case, for one, you're a naive and idealistic schoolteacher who's been kept out of the loop."

"Well, at least I've improved in your estimation in the last fifteen years." She dropped her handbag onto a chair. If she couldn't sit, at least she could get rid of some dead weight while she faced Cole. "That's more than you would have said about me in high school."

"At this point I have a good sense of when you're to blame," he shot back, not answering directly.

"Meaning you have plenty of experience?"

Cole gave her a penetrating look and then said, "Here's what you're going to do. You're going to tell the principal—"

"Mr. Dobson."

"—that you've got me on board for the fund-raiser, but there's one condition attached."

"Serenghetti Construction gets the job."

Marisa had been on a roller coaster of emotions since walking into Cole's office. And right now elation that Cole was agreeing to be her headliner threatened to overwhelm everything else. She tried to appear calm but a part of her wanted to jump up and down with relief.

Cole nodded, seemingly oblivious to her emotional state. "Let Dobson deal with the board of directors. My guess is that the member with ties to JM Construction will have to back down. If Dobson plays his cards right, he'll marshal support even before the next board meeting."

"And if he doesn't?"

"He will, especially if I say Jordan will show up, too, even though he's not a graduate of the school. Pershing isn't a public school that's legally bound to accept the lowest bid on a contract. And giving the contract to Serenghetti Construction makes sense. The money that the school would save not having to pay a big name to appear at their fund-raiser tips the balance on the bottom line."

She sighed. "You've thought of everything."

"Not everything. I still have to deal with you, sweet pea."

His words hurt, but she managed to keep her expression even. "Bad luck."

"Bad luck comes in threes. Getting injured, needing to take over a construction firm, you showing up..."

"We're even," she parried. "I've been cheated on, gotten dumped by my fiancé and had to recruit you for the fund-raiser."

He smiled, and she thought she detected a spark of admiration for her willingness to meet him head-on. "Not so diplomatic now that you know you have me hooked."

"Only because you're willing to be ruthless with your competitors."

"Just like your douche bag fiancé?" he asked. "How did you wind up engaged to Sal? Are you hanging out in sports bars these days?"

"You know from personal experience that I visit boxing gyms." She shrugged. "Why not a sports bar?"

His eyes crinkled. "You showed up at Jimmy's only because you were tracking me. You'd probably claim your appearance was under duress."

"I'm not going to argue."

"You're not?" he quipped. "What a change."

"You're welcome."

His expression sobered. "For the record, you don't know what to wear to a gym."

"I came from school dressed like a teacher," she protested.

His eyes swept over her. "Exactly. As I said, you're a walking cliché."

"And you are frustrating and irritating." She spoke lightly, but she sort of meant it, too.

"Talk to my opponents on the ice. They'll tell you all about it."

"I'm sure they would."

"It's nice to know I bother you, sweet pea."

Their gazes caught and held, and awareness coiled through her, threatening to break free. She wet her lips, and Cole's eyes moved to her mouth.

"Are you still pining and crying your eyes out for him?" he asked abruptly.

She blinked, caught off guard. She wasn't going to admit as much to Cole of all people, but she'd done enough pining and crying in high school to last a lifetime. Still, it would be pathetic if she'd met and lost the love of her life at eighteen. Her life couldn't have ended that early.

"For whom?" she asked carefully.

"Piazza."

"Not really."

She'd dated since graduating from Pershing, but nothing had panned out past a few dates until Sal. It was as if she'd needed to lick her wounds for a long time after high school—after Cole.

There'd been initial shock over Sal's betrayal, of course. But then she'd gotten on with her life. She had a low opinion of Sal, and she was still angry about being cheated on. But she wasn't lying in bed wondering how she was going to go on—or wishing Sal would see the light and come back to her.

She'd been prepared to be hit by the despair that had assailed her after her teenage fling with Cole. So either she'd matured, or her relationship with Sal hadn't been as significant as she'd told herself. She refused to analyze which was the case.

Cole shrugged. "Piazza isn't worth it. He's a cheating a—"

"You've never cheated on a woman?" They were getting into personal territory, but she couldn't stop herself from asking the question.

Cole assumed a set expression. "I've dated plenty, but it's always been serial. And you never answered my question about how you met Piazza."

"Why are you interested?" she shot back before sighing in resignation. "We did meet in a bar, actually. Some teachers met for Friday night drinks, and I was persuaded to go along. He was an acquaintance of an acquaintance…"

Cole arched an eyebrow, as if prompting her for more.

"He was steady, reliable…"

"A bedrock to build a marriage on. But he turned out to be so reliable, he cheated on you."

"What do you suggest constructing a lasting relationship on?" she lobbed back. "A hormone-fueled hookup with a woman as deep as a puddle after a light rain?"

She didn't pose the question as if it was about him in particular, but he could read between the lines.

"I haven't even tried for more. That's the difference."

"As I said, Sal appeared steady and reliable…" And

she'd been desperate for the respectably ordinary. All she'd wanted as an adult was to be middle class, with a Cape Cod or a split level in the suburbs and a couple of kids…and *no money worries.*

Sal had grown up in Welsdale, too, but unlike her, he'd attended Welsdale High School, so they hadn't known each other as teenagers. When they'd met, he'd been working for a Springfield-based sports management company, but was often back in his hometown, which was where they had gotten acquainted one night at The Obelisk Lounge. Sal traveled to Boston regularly for business, but he and his firm mainly focused on trolling the waters of professional hockey at the Springfield arena where the New England Razors played.

Cole looked irritated. "Sal is the sports version of a used car salesman—always preparing to pitch you the next deal as if it's the best thing since sliced bread."

"As far as I can tell, a lot of you sports pros believe you are the best thing since sliced bread."

They were skimming the surface of the deep lake of emotion and past history between them. Every encounter with Cole was an emotional wringer. You'd think she'd be used to it by now or at least expecting it.

Cole shrugged. "Hockey is a job."

"So is teaching."

"It's the reason you made your way back to Pershing."

"The school was good to me." She shifted and then picked up her handbag.

Cole didn't move. "I'll bet. How long have you been teaching there?"

"I started right after college, so not quite ten years." She took a step toward the door and then paused. "It took me more than five years and several part-time jobs to get my degree and provisional teaching certificate at U. Mass. Amherst."

She could see she'd surprised him. She'd gone to a state school, where the tuition had been lower and she'd qualified for a scholarship. Even then, though, because she'd been more or less self-supporting, it had taken a while to get her degree. She'd worked an odd and endless assortment of jobs: telemarketer, door-to-door sales rep, supermarket checkout clerk and receptionist.

She knew Cole had gone on to Boston College, which was a powerhouse in college hockey. She was sure he hadn't had to hold down two part-time jobs in order to graduate, but she gave him credit if he continued to work in the family construction business, as he'd done at Pershing.

"I remember you didn't have much money in high school," he said.

"I was a scholarship student. I worked summers and sometimes weekends scooping ice cream at the Ben & Jerry's on Sycamore St."

"Yeah, I remember."

She remembered, too. *Oh, did she remember.* Cole and the rest of his jock posse had hardly ever set foot in the store, but it had been a favorite of teenage girls. She'd waited on her classmates, and usually it had worked out okay, but a few stuck-up types had enjoyed queening it over her. Cole had stopped in during the brief time they'd been study buddies...

"And you worked summers at Serenghetti Construction," she said unnecessarily, suddenly nervous because they weren't squabbling anymore.

"All the way through college."

"But you didn't have to do it for the money."

"No, not for the money," he responded, "but there are different shades of *have to*. There's the *have to* that comes with family obligation."

"Is that why you're back and running Serenghetti Construction?"

He nodded curtly. "At least temporarily. I've got other opportunities on the back burner."

She tried to hide her surprise. "You're planning to play hockey again?"

"No, but there are other options. Coaching, for instance."

Her heart fell, but Marisa told herself not to be ridiculous even as she fidgeted with her handbag strap. She didn't care what Cole Serenghetti's plans were, and she shouldn't be surprised they didn't involve staying in Welsdale and heading Serenghetti Construction.

"How is your father doing?" she asked, trying to bring the conversation back to safer ground. News of Serg's stroke was public knowledge around Welsdale.

"He's doing therapy to regain some motor function."

Marisa didn't say anything, sensing that Cole might continue if she remained silent.

"It's doubtful he'll be able to run Serenghetti Construction again."

"That must be tough." If Serg didn't recover more, and Cole had no plans to head the family business on a permanent basis, Marisa wondered what would happen. Would one of Cole's brothers step in to head the company? But Jordan was having an impressive run with the Razors… She contained her curiosity, because Cole had been a closed door to her for fifteen years— and she liked it that way, she told herself.

"Dad's a fighter. We'll see what happens," Cole said, seeming like a man who rarely, if ever, invited sympathy. "He's joked about the lengths he'll go to retire and hand over the reins to one of his kids."

She smiled, and Cole's expression relaxed.

"How's your mother?" he asked, appearing okay with chitchat about their families.

"She recently married a carpenter." Ted Millepied was a good man who adored her mother.

Cole quirked his lips. "Where's he based? I may be able to use him."

"You don't believe in guilt by association?" The words left her mouth before she could stop them, but she was surprised that Cole would even consider hiring someone related to her by marriage.

Cole sobered. "No, despite what my cockamamie brother may have led you to believe about the Serenghettis and the labeling of relationships to the nth degree of separation."

Jordan's words came back to her. *Entangled by proxy? Engaged by one degree of separation?* In fact, there was no connection between her and Cole. She refused to believe in any. There'd only been dead air since high school.

"My mother is still in Welsdale," she elaborated. "She's worked her way up to management at Stanhope Department Store. In fact, she recently got named buyer for housewares."

She was proud of her mother. After many years in retail, earning college credit at night and on weekends, Donna Casale had been rewarded with management-track promotions at Stanhope, which anchored the biggest shopping center in the Welsdale area. The store was where Marisa's wealthier classmates at Pershing had bought many of their clothes—and where Marisa had gotten by with her mother's employee discounts.

Cole was looking at her closely, and she gave herself a mental shake. They had drifted deep into personal stuff. *Stop, stop, stop.* She should get going. "Okay," she said briskly, "if Pershing meets your terms about the construction job, will you do the fund-raiser?"

Cole looked alert. "Yes."

"Wonderful." She stepped forward and held out her hand. "It's a deal."

Cole enveloped Marisa's hand, and sensation swamped her. Their eyes met, and the moment dragged out between them... He was so close, she could see the sprinkling of gold in his irises. She'd also forgotten how tall Cole was, because she'd limited herself to the occasional glimpse of him on television or in print for the past fifteen years.

She swallowed, her lips parting.

Cole dropped his gaze to her mouth. "Did you mean what you said to Jordan?"

"Wh-what?" She cleared her throat and tried again. "What in particular?"

"Was he your Plan B?"

"I don't have a Plan B."

"What about regretting telling on me to Mr. Hayes in high school?"

The world shrank to include only the two of them. "Every day. I wished circumstances had been different."

"Ever wish things had turned out differently between us?"

"Yes."

"Yeah, me too."

A cell phone buzzed, breaking the moment.

Marisa stepped back, and Cole reached into his pocket.

"Mr. Serenghetti?"

Marisa glanced toward the door and saw the receptionist.

"I've got it," Cole said. "He phoned my cell."

The receptionist nodded as she retreated. "Your four o'clock is here, too."

Cole held Marisa's gaze as he addressed whoever was on the other end of the line. From what Marisa could tell, the call was about a materials delivery for one of Serenghetti's construction sites.

But it was the message that she read in Cole's expression that captured her attention. *Later. We're not done yet.*

Marisa gave a quick nod before turning and heading for the door.

As she made her way past reception, down in the elevator and out the building, she pondered Cole's words about wishing things had worked out differently between them. What had he meant? And did it matter?

But there was more to puzzle over in his expression. *We're not done.*

It was more than had existed between them in fifteen years—or maybe they were just going to write a different ending.

Four

Marisa gazed up at him with big, wide eyes. "Please, Cole. I want you."

"Yes," he heard himself answer, his voice thick.

They were made to fit together. He'd waited fifteen years to show her how good it could be between them. He wanted to tell her that he would please her. This would be no crazy fumble on a sofa. When it came to sex, their communication had the potential to be flawless and explosive.

He claimed her lips and traced the seam of her mouth. She opened for him, tasting sweet as a ripe berry, and then met his tongue. The kiss deepened and gained urgency. They pressed together, and she moaned.

He felt the pressing need of his arousal as her breasts pushed against his chest. She was sexy and hot, and she wanted him. He'd never felt this deep need for anyone else. It was primitive and basic and...right.

"Oh, Cole." She looked at him, her eyes wide amber pools. "Please. Now."

"Yes," he said hoarsely. "It's going to be so good between us, sweet pea. I promise."

He positioned himself, and then held her gaze as he pushed inside her. She was warm and slick and tight. And he was sliding toward mindless rapture...

Cole awoke with a start.

Glancing around, half-dazed, he realized he was restless, aroused—and alone.

He sprawled across his king-size bed, where damp sheets had ridden down his bare chest and tangled around his legs. Most of all, there was the feeling of being irritated and unfulfilled.

Damn it.

He'd been fantasizing about Marisa Danieli. He'd itched to ride her curves and have her come apart in his arms. He worked hard to slow his pounding pulse and then threw off the sheets. A glance at the bedside clock told him he needed to be at the office in an hour. He hit the alarm before it could go off and then rose and headed to the shower.

The master suite in his Welsdale condo included a large marble bath and a walk-in closet. He'd bought the place—on the top floor of a prewar building in the center of downtown—in order to have a home base during his hockey career. Not to mention that like the rest of the Serenghettis, he was a keen real estate investor.

The condo had been a place where he could retreat during the off-season without becoming an extended houseguest of his parents. His brothers kept places nearby, while his sister preferred to stay at Casa Serenghetti—as the siblings sometimes jokingly referred to the family manse—when she was in town.

He opened the glass door to the shower stall and then stood under the lukewarm spray, waiting for it to cool him down before he grabbed a bar of soap and lathered up.

He told himself he'd been dreaming about Marisa only because he wanted to win. Sex was just a metaphor for crashing through her defenses. Then he'd have some relief from this frustrating dance that they were engaged in.

Certainly he didn't want a round two with her. He wasn't even sure he trusted her...

After dressing, he made the quick drive to his office at Serenghetti Construction. He'd just reached his desk when the receptionist announced that she had Mr. Dobson from the Pershing School on the phone.

Interesting. It appeared Marisa had spoken with Pershing's principal, and Mr. Dobson was wasting no time getting the wheels turning on his end.

Through careful questioning of his contacts, Cole had learned that a Pershing board member was golf buddies with the CEO of JM Construction. He didn't have solid evidence that JM Construction had been a shoo-in for building the gym, but it was enough. In the end, proof didn't matter anyway. He needed that job to go to Serenghetti Construction and not JM.

"Mr. Dobson, Cole Serenghetti here. What can I do for you?" Cole made his voice sound detached, even a bit bored.

Dobson engaged in pleasantries for a few minutes, as if he and Cole already knew each other and the call was an ordinary occurrence. Then without missing a beat, the principal thanked him for agreeing to head-line Pershing Shines Bright, and invited Serenghetti Construction to submit a proposal for building the gym.

Cole leaned back in his chair. Since coming to his office last week, Marisa must have delivered the message at Pershing that the fund-raiser and the construction job were a package deal. Still, he needed to make sure there was no doubt about this understanding. He expected at least a handshake deal, if not a signed contract, before the school benefit took place.

Drawing on the business savvy that he'd gotten at an early age by observing Serg, Cole said, "I have an architectural partnership that I work with. I suggest setting up a meeting for next week where we can discuss the vision for the new gym as well as talk about costs and the timeline. Afterward, I'll submit contracts for your review."

Dobson paused a beat and then heartily agreed with Cole's suggestion.

"Feel free to invite any of the directors on your board to the meeting next week," Cole continued. "I want each and every one of them to be comfortable with the Serenghetti team."

There was another beat before the principal responded. "I can assure you that the board couldn't have been more pleased to hear the Serenghetti name mentioned in connection with both the fund-raiser and the construction of the gym. They need no reassurance."

Cole smiled, glad that he and Dobson understood each other. Clearly, the principal was savvy himself. He appeared to have done the math and realized that a *free* appearance by a hockey star or two was worth plenty to the school's bottom line. Cole made a mental note to call Jordan and tell him that *both* of them would be showing up for Pershing Shines Bright.

Thinking he needed to do Marisa a favor for keeping her word, Cole went on, "Invite Ms. Danieli to the meeting, too. If she's in charge of the fund-raiser, she'll need to be able to speak knowledgeably to potential donors about the building project."

"Excellent idea," Dobson concurred. "I will let her know."

As soon as his conversation with the principal had ended, Cole called his youngest brother and put him on speakerphone.

"Put the Pershing School benefit on your calendar," he told Jordan without prelude. "I'll email you the date and time when I get them from Marisa. You and I will be making an appearance in our best penguin suits or closest equivalent."

As he spoke, he opened a blank email and began drafting a message to Marisa. Did she have a black-tie event in mind? He hadn't concerned himself with the details up to now. He also needed to tell her that Jordan would be participating, too. He didn't pause now to analyze why he was relishing communicating with her, even if just by email, after the dead air between them since she'd shown up at his office.

Jordan's unmistakable chuckle sounded over the phone line. "First, you told me to stay away from Marisa, now you want me to attend her fund-raiser with you. Which is it? And more important, will you be a good date?"

Cole figured he should have expected Jordan's needling. "You wouldn't be my date for the fund-raiser, numbskull."

"Why, Cole," his brother cooed, "you do know how to break someone's heart. Did I lose out to Marisa, or is there another teacher who's gotten you hot under the collar lately?"

"Later, Jordan." Cole punched the button to end the call.

He finished his email, and then, after finding an address for Marisa on Pershing's website, fired it off.

Leaning back in his chair again, he allowed himself momentary satisfaction at cutting off JM Construction. Now all he needed to do was wait for Marisa to come calling with the details…

The second time wasn't as intimidating, Marisa thought, as she walked through Serenghetti Construction's offices on a Thursday afternoon.

Last week she'd sat in on a meeting between Mr. Dobson and Cole and his architectural firm to discuss the contract to build Pershing's gym. The talk had been about use requirements, building permits and environmental impact. Then there'd been a discussion of hardwood, maple grades, subflooring, HVAC systems and disability access. Marisa had jotted notes to keep up with the onslaught of details. She'd been aware of Cole's gaze on her from time to time as he'd talked, but she'd kept her head down and stayed in the background, asking only a couple of questions.

She was a teacher, not a builder, but she'd known as soon as the meeting was over that she would have to do some serious studying if she hoped one day to be an assistant principal. School administrators like

Mr. Dobson had more on their plate than the curriculum. They were also responsible for the physical condition of the school buildings that they oversaw.

In fact, she had done a little online research this past weekend because today she had to deal with Cole all by herself. She was supposed to look at architectural plans and give her input to Mr. Dobson. The principal had asked her to look at the plans for other athletic facilities built by Serenghetti Construction.

She should be happy about her expanded responsibilities because maybe it was a sign that Mr. Dobson would consider her for a promotion. But instead, her thoughts were on Cole. Since their meeting last week, her communication with him had been limited. They'd exchanged brief emails about the time and place of the fund-raiser, and he'd signed off on the use of his bio and photo.

But her active imagination had filled in what had been left unsaid. She'd gone over every look and word that Cole had given her during their meeting with Mr. Dobson and the architect. She'd also replayed their last conversation at his office—especially the part about wishing their relationship had turned out differently.

She was grateful to him for agreeing to do the fund-raiser. And *vulnerable* and *attracted*…

Danger, danger, danger… She could never become involved with Cole. *Not with her family history.* She'd lived with the consequences of the past her whole life, even if she hadn't known the details until her twenties.

Bringing herself back to the present, she gave her name to the receptionist, who directed her toward Cole's office with little fanfare.

When she reached Cole's door, he looked up, as if sensing her there.

"Marisa." He stood and came around his desk.

Her pulse picked up, and she stepped into the room, resisting the urge to hug her light blazer to her instead of leaving it draped over one arm. As usual, she was hit with an overwhelming awareness of him as a man. Today he was dressed in a suit but he had shed his jacket and tie. Still, even though he wasn't in full corporate uniform, he appeared every inch the successful and wealthy business executive.

Marisa shifted. She'd dressed in a striped shirt and navy pants—an appropriate and understated outfit in her opinion. She dared him to take note of her clothing one more time and call her a cliché.

Cole's eyes surveyed her as he approached, but he said nothing.

Did she imagine that he lingered at the V created by her shirt, his gaze flickering with heat for a moment? It was like being touched by a feather—light, and yet packed with sensation.

When he stopped in front of her, he asked without preamble, "What did you think of our meeting with Dobson last week?"

She resisted saying she thought of it as her and Mr. Dobson's meeting with *him*. "It went well."

Cole nodded. "Dobson wants you to see some older plans today. Every job is unique, but I'm guessing he wants to cover his bases and have you do some due diligence."

"In case he needs to account for the way the construction contract with Serenghetti came about?"

Cole gave her a dry look and inclined his head.

"You'll be the one doing the explaining since you're here today. You're going to get a sense of what past clients have gone with."

"Okay." She really was in the hot seat. "Do you have plans for other gyms that Serenghetti has built?"

"One or two." Cole arched a brow. "You might as well get acquainted with the nitty-gritty of construction. Nobody plays around here. Least of all me." He pulled his office door open wider and indicated she should precede him out of the room. "You can leave your stuff here. We'll be back in a few minutes."

Marisa dropped her handbag and blazer on a chair and then walked beside Cole down the corridor and around the corner.

Stopping in front of an older-looking door, Cole retrieved keys from his pocket and opened two different dead bolts.

"I guess not everything at Serenghetti Construction is state-of-the-art," she remarked lightly.

Cole quirked his lips. "The new Pershing gym will be, don't worry. This building dates back to the 1930s, and we kept the old-fashioned storage room with concrete walls and dead bolts. It's where we keep confidential files and old documents."

He opened the door and flipped the light switch.

Marisa saw a small room lined with metal cabinets. A walkable strip down the middle extended about seven or eight feet into the room.

Cole moved inside, and Marisa watched as he scanned the cabinets.

"There must be a few decades' worth of files in there."

"Building rehabilitation is a substantial share of our

business," Cole answered, glancing back at her. "We refer to these plans when we do renovations or additions to existing structures, either for returning clients or new owners."

"I see."

He looked amused. "Come on in."

Reluctantly, she let go of the door and stepped inside. She let her gaze travel over the cabinets because the alternative was allowing it to settle on Cole. The labels on the metal drawers were a mystery to her. "How do you know where to look?"

Then, hearing a click behind her, she turned to see that the door had creaked shut. Pushing aside a prick of panic, she said, "I'll, uh, step back out to give you more room to search for what you're looking for."

She grasped the door handle and tried to turn it. The door, however, didn't budge. She jiggled the handle again and pushed.

"Now you've done it."

She swung around, her eyes widening. "What do you mean?"

"You've locked us in."

She gave him an accusatory look. "You told me to step inside!"

"But not to let the door close behind you. There's a doorstop outside. Didn't you see it?"

"No!"

"Are you afraid of small spaces?" he asked sardonically.

"Don't be ridiculous." She had a fear of *Cole and small spaces*.

"Breathe."

"I don't want to suck all of the air out of the room."

He looked as if he was stifling a laugh. "You won't. Does this happen often?"

"It comes and goes," she admitted. "I'm not claustrophobic, but I'm not a big fan of tiny areas, either."

"Relax."

She sent up a prayer because she was in sensory overload right now, and his nearness in the closet-like space threatened to short-circuit her. "You're finding this amusing, aren't you?"

"Vasovagal syncope, claustrophobia… It keeps getting better and better with you."

"Very funny." She'd never put her best foot forward with him. She felt exposed, her vulnerabilities on display.

"You could scream for help," he suggested. "It might suck all the air out of the room, so think about whether you're willing to go for broke…"

"The only reason to scream is because you're making me crazy."

He stepped toward her, bringing them within brushing distance. "There's always your cell phone."

"I left it in your office along with my handbag." She perked up. "What about your phone?"

"Ditto except for the part about the handbag."

She lowered her shoulders. "How could you let this happen?"

"I didn't," he said with exaggerated patience.

She grasped at any topic she could in order to take her mind off her panic. "Did you ever think that Serenghetti Construction might be your second career after hockey someday?"

"No, but I have a construction background, thanks to working summers at Serenghetti Construction to earn money. I majored in management at Boston College, but I also took community college classes in bid estimating, drafting and blueprint reading that helped at the summer jobs."

"Because your father always wanted you to succeed him at Serenghetti Construction."

"Someone had to, but I never committed."

"And then your hockey dreams were cut short."

He gave her a droll look. "For a woman who doesn't like to confront uncomfortable topics, you sure don't mince words."

She frowned. "What topics don't I like to talk about? I'm just wondering whether it may have been hard to come to terms with your new situation."

He folded his arms. "Like you haven't come to grips with the past?"

"What do you mean?" *He was way too close.*

"Us."

"Some of us weren't lucky enough to have a Plan B that involved a job in the family business."

His gaze sharpened. "Oh no, you don't. I'm not letting you avoid the topic. Why did you go to Mr. Hayes with the story that I pulled the prank? Because I came from money and had a Plan B?"

"Please," she scoffed.

He was too close, too much, too everything.

The school assembly during their senior year had been named Pershing Does Good. It was supposed to have been video highlights of the Pershing community doing volunteer work. Instead, it had turned into a joke because Cole had inserted images of Mr. Hayes's head superimposed on a champion wrestler's body, and one of the principal seemingly dressed only in boxers and socks and posing next to a convertible.

It had been a brilliant piece of hacking, but Mr. Hayes had been in no mood to laugh.

Cole moved closer. "Or was it a way to get back at me after we'd had sex and I didn't shower you with pretty phrases?"

She made a sound of disbelief. "You didn't talk to me, either."

He paused, his eyes gleaming. "Ah, now we're getting somewhere."

"Where?" she demanded. "You've written a script about a jilted lover seeking revenge."

"Weren't you one?"

"I was a virgin."

"Okay, so I was the evil seducer who stole your virginity, and hell hath no fury like a woman scorned? That's a good story, too, except my recollection is that you were a willing participant."

She shook her head vehemently. "It had nothing to do with sex. At least my confession to Mr. Hayes didn't. You were closer when you thought it had to do with money."

Cole's face hardened.

"Mr. Hayes called me into his office. He guessed there were seniors who knew more about the prank than he did." She fought to keep her voice even. "So he pulled in the person he thought he had something to hold over. Namely, me."

Cole scowled.

"You humiliated and embarrassed him in front of the whole student body. He was going to get to the bottom of it, come hell or high water. So he threatened to take away my recommendation for a college scholarship unless I confessed who did it." She swallowed. "I'd overheard you telling one of your teammates near the lockers that you'd managed to sneak into the school offices."

Marisa had known back then in the principal's office that Mr. Hayes's job was at stake. While working her after-school job sweeping hallways, she'd overheard conversations among the staff about the principal's contract maybe not being renewed by Pershing's board because there was debate about Mr. Hayes's performance. Cole's prank would further make it seem as if Mr. Hayes wasn't a good leader who commanded the respect of the school community.

Marisa had looked at Mr. Hayes, and in that instant, she'd read his thoughts. He was worried because his career might be on the line, and he had three kids to support at home. She had been able to relate because her mother had stressed about her job, too, and she'd had only one kid to worry about.

Cole's frown faded, and then his eyes narrowed.

"I was backed into a corner. I had no Plan B. I needed that scholarship money, or there would be no happy ending for me. At least not one involving college in the fall."

Cole's lips thinned. "It's unconscionable that the bastard would have twisted the arm of an eighteen-year-old student."

"I was on scholarship at Pershing. I was there on condition of good grades and better behavior. Unlike some people, I didn't have the luxury of being a prankster."

Cole swore.

"So you were right all along. I did sell you out, and I'm sorry." She felt the wind leave her, her words slowing after spilling in a mad rush. "If it helps, I was ostracized. People saw me go in and out of Mr. Hayes's office, so they guessed who ratted you out. After all, you got confronted by Mr. Hayes right after I was interrogated, so the rumors started immediately. My only defense was that if I hadn't kept my scholarship, I'd probably have struggled to make ends meet like my mother. I knew college was my ticket out."

She ought to stop talking but she couldn't help herself. The words had come out in a torrent and were now down to a trickle, but she couldn't seem to turn off the flow completely.

"Why didn't you tell me back then about Hayes blackmailing you into a confession?" Cole demanded. "He let slip your name when he confronted me, but he never got into details."

"Would you have been ready to listen?" she replied. "All you cared about was the Independent School League championship. My reasons didn't make a difference. You still wouldn't have been able to play the end of the season."

The old hurts from high school came back vividly, and she felt a throbbing pain in the region of her heart. She'd stayed home on the night of the prom. She and Serafina had watched Molly Ringwald flicks from the '80s. The high school angst on the television screen had fit Marisa's mood—because she'd been into self-flagellation. She'd discovered that Cole—his suspension ended—was going to the prom with Kendra Vance, a cheerleader. She'd cried herself to sleep long after Sera's head had hit the pillow, hiding her grief because she didn't want to invite questions from her cousin.

Marisa sucked in a trembling breath while Cole stared at her, his expression inscrutable. She realized she'd hurt him, and now he was still wary. But there was no way to change the past.

"How are we getting out of here?" she asked, reverting to her earlier panic—because, strangely, it seemed safer territory than the one she'd ventured into with Cole.

Flustered, she gestured randomly until Cole captured her hands. He gave her a look of such intensity, it stole her breath.

"Now would be the time to scream, I think," he said.

"Because we're out of options?"

"No. Because if I haven't made you crazy already, this will."

Then he bent his head and captured her mouth, swallowing her gasp.

Cole folded her into his arms. He kissed her with a self-assurance that sent chills of awareness chasing through her. She felt his hard muscles pressed against her soft curves. Her breasts tingled. *Everything* tingled.

He savored her mouth, stroking her lips until they were wet and plump and prickling with need. His tongue darted to the seam of her lips, and she opened for him. He moved his hands up to cup her head and thread his fingers in her hair. Then he stroked inside her mouth, deepening the kiss, and she met him instinctively. She sighed, and he made a sound of satisfaction.

She wanted him. She'd developed a crush on him in high school, and she still felt an attraction for him that would not be denied. Longing, nervousness and defenselessness mixed in a heady concoction.

Slowly, Cole eased back and then broke off the kiss.

Marisa opened her eyes and met Cole's glittering look.

"That did it."

"Wh-what?" she responded, her voice husky.

"You forgot about being panicked."

He was only partly right. She'd forgotten about the small space they were stuck in, all right. But she'd replaced that anxiety with a sexual awareness of him.

She took a small step back and felt the cabinets press up against her. Frowning, and seeking composure, she asked, "How can you kiss a woman you don't even like?"

"You needed a kiss right then."

She flushed. "What I need is to get out of here."

He moved past her and she tensed. One little push and she'd be back in his arms.

She turned and watched him grasp the door handle and turn it hard. At the same time, he shoved his shoulder against the door—once, twice… The door swung open.

Turning back, he smiled faintly. "After you."

She stepped into the hallway with no small relief. Still, she found herself tossing him an accusatory look. "You knew all along that it would open, didn't you?"

"I knew there was nothing stopping it, except maybe a little stickiness from age. Simple deductive logic. It would have occurred to you, too, if you hadn't been panicked and babbling."

"When I think I'm about to suffocate to death, the words flow." Now the only threat to her life was death by embarrassment. What had she confessed? And she'd melted into his arms… "I've got to go. I—I'm sorry. We'll need to reschedule."

"Marisa…"

She backed up a few steps and then turned and walked rapidly down the hall, not waiting for him to lock the storage room. She stopped only to grab her jacket and handbag from Cole's office as she made her way out the building and to her car.

She'd already consoled herself with chocolate cake—what was left?

Five

Cole perused the job site from where he was standing on a muddy rise. His mind was only half on the discussion that he needed to have with his foreman. The other half was on what he had to do about Marisa.

Unlike the construction project in Springfield where Marisa had waylaid him, this one was already at the stage where drywall and electrical had gone in. But he needed to get updates from his crew and hammer out remaining issues so they could come in under budget and on time. The five-story office complex outside Northampton was another one of their big projects.

"Sam is coming down now!" one of his construction crew called.

Cole gave him a brief nod before his thoughts were set adrift again.

He'd put in a call to Pershing's principal soon after

Marisa had fled his offices several days ago. He'd covered for her by taking the heat for their meeting falling through. Hell, it was the least he could do after finding out the truth about fifteen years ago. And, he was willing to humor Pershing's principal to get the job done. Never mind that he thought reviewing the plans for prior construction jobs was a waste of time. Every job was unique; everybody knew as much.

Still, he hadn't been able to stop thinking about Marisa. All these years he'd hated her. *No, that wasn't right.* He'd built up a wall and sealed her off from the rest of his life.

Now he understood the choice that Marisa had faced in the principal's office. And yeah, she'd been right on target about the way he'd been in high school. He wouldn't have wanted to hear her confession. Because he'd been a callow eighteen-year-old to whom a high school championship had meant more than it should.

In contrast, Marisa had been an insightful teen. She'd shown that understanding when it had come to Mr. Hayes, and Cole had spurned her for it. But the truth was, Cole had fallen for her back then precisely because she'd seemed self-possessed and different. She'd stood outside the usual shallow preoccupations of their classmates. The truth was she'd been more mature—no doubt because she'd had to grow up fast.

Cole cursed silently.

Marisa had been wrong about one thing, though. *All you cared about was the hockey championship.* He'd cared about her, too…until he'd felt betrayed.

In the storage room, she'd looked at him with her limpid big brown eyes, and he'd stopped himself from touching her face to reassure her. He was sure that if he'd reached for her pulse right then, it would have jumped under his touch.

Then she'd rocked him with her explanation about being called to the mat by Mr. Hayes, and he'd kissed her. The lip-lock had been as good as he'd fantasized, and even better than his memory of high school. She had a way of slipping under his skin and making him hunger…

His pulse started to hum at the thought…and at the anticipation of seeing her again. He just needed to make it happen.

He took out his phone and started typing a text message. She'd called from her cell phone when she'd needed to set up the meeting at Serenghetti's offices to review construction plans, and he'd made note of the number.

Told Dobson our meeting cut short b/c I had other business. Let's reschedule. Dinner Friday @6. LMK.

As soon as he hit Send, he felt his spirits lift.

Spotting his foreman coming toward him, he slipped the phone into the back pocket of his jeans and adjusted his hard hat. There was unfinished business today, and there would be unfinished business on Friday. But first he had a meeting today that was a long time coming.

As soon as his consultation with the foreman was over, Cole drove to his parents' house. He made his way to the back garden, where he knew he'd find his parents, based on what his mother had told him during his call to her earlier.

Serg was ensconced in a wrought-iron chair. Bundled in a jacket and blanket against the nippy air, he looked as if he was dressed for an Alaskan sledding event. Because if there was one thing that Camilla Serenghetti feared, it was someone dear to her *catching a chilly*, as she liked to say. It came second only to the fear that her husband or one of her kids might go hungry. She hovered near a small round patio table littered with a display of fruit, bread, water and tea.

Cole took a seat and began with easy chitchat. Fortunately, the stroke had not affected his father's speech. The conversation touched on Serg's health before veering toward other mundane topics. All the while, however, his father appeared grumpy and tense—as if he sensed there was another purpose to this visit.

Holding back a grimace, Cole took his chance when the talk reached a lull. "I'm looking for buyers for the business."

Serg hit the table with his fist. "Over my dead body."

Cole resisted the urge to point out that it might well come to that—another stroke and Serg was finished. "We're a midsize construction company. Our best bet is a buyout by one of the big players."

Then Cole could get on with his life. Nothing had panned out yet, but there were coaching positions available, and he wanted to grow the business investment portfolio he'd begun to put together thanks to his NHL earnings.

"Never."

"It's not good for you to get upset in your condition, Dad." He'd thought he could have a rational discussion with his father about the future of Serenghetti Construction, because Serg was never going to make a one-hundred-percent recovery. So unless Serenghetti

Construction was sold, Cole wouldn't just be a temporary caretaker of the company, but a permanent fixture.

"You know what's not good for me? My son talking about selling the company that I broke my back to build."

Camilla rushed forward. "Lie back against the pillows. Don't upset yourself."

"Dad, be reasonable." Cole fought to keep his frustration at bay. He'd waited months to have this conversation with his father. But now everyone had to face reality. Serg was not going to show more significant improvement. Maybe he could enjoy a productive retirement, but the chances that he'd be fit to head a demanding business again were slim. The discussion about the future had to start now.

"What's wrong with the company that you want to sell it?"

"It needs to grow or die."

"And you're not interested in growing it?"

Cole let silence be his answer.

"I heard you outmaneuvered JM to get the contract to build a new gym at the Pershing School."

Cole figured Serg had been informed about the gym contract on one of his occasional phone calls to Serenghetti Construction's head offices. His father liked to speak to senior employees and stay clued in on what was going on beyond what Cole had time to tell him. Cole had told no one at the office about his bargain with Marisa beyond the fact that Serenghetti Construction had managed to stay a step ahead of its competitor JM Construction.

"Grow or die!" Serg gestured as if there was an audience aside from Camilla. "This company paid for your college degree and your hockey training. There's nothing wrong with it."

"Serenghetti Construction is not the little train that could, Dad." The company needed fresh blood at the helm in order to steer it into the future. Serg, like many founders, had taken it as far as he could. And if Cole wasn't careful, he himself would be captaining the ship for decades ahead.

"So what are you going to do instead that's more important?" Serg groused, shifting in his chair and nearly knocking over his cane. "Go be a hockey coach?"

Cole wasn't surprised his father guessed the direction of his thoughts. He'd interviewed for a coaching job with the Madison Rockets last fall, but having heard nothing further, he'd kept the news to himself. If a position materialized, there was no question that his time at the helm of Serenghetti Construction would need to come to an end because he couldn't keep jobs in different states—not to mention the travel involved in a coaching position.

Serg snapped his brows together. "Coaching is a hard lifestyle if you have a family and a couple of kids." He glowered. "Or is that something else you're planning to do differently from the old man? Another part of your heritage that you're planning to reject?"

"Getting married and having kids is hardly part of my heritage, Dad." More like a lifestyle choice, but Serg had jumped ahead several steps.

"Well, we damn sure don't speak the same language anymore! How's that for losing your heritage?"

"Serg, calm down," Camilla said, looking worried. "You know what the *dottore* said."

Camilla had always been the one to run interference between her husband and children. Cole also had a hunch that his mother had more empathy than his father about lifelong dreams and their postponement. His mother had her own second career as a television chef.

"The blood thinners will take care of me—" Serg harrumphed before shooting Cole a pointed look "—even if my children won't."

"I'll take care of you," Camilla said firmly.

Cole looked at his parents. "Well, this is a turn-around."

Serg frowned. "What? Stop speaking in riddles."

Cole wasn't sure his pronouncement would be welcome. "Suddenly Mom is the one with a career, and she's promising to support you."

"You always were a smart aleck," his father grumbled. "Maybe even a bigger one than your brother."

"Which one?" Cole quipped—because both Jordan and Rick qualified—and then stood up. "I'm going to let you continue to rest. I have a couple of calls to return for work."

"Rest! That's all anyone wants me to do around here."

Cole figured if he could rest, he'd be ahead of the game right now. But he had demands on his time, not the least of which was a certain wild-tressed schoolteacher who'd come crashing back into his life…

"Hi, Mom."

"Honey!" Donna Casale rushed forward, delight stamped on her face as she left her front door wide open behind her.

For Marisa, it was like looking at an older version of herself. Fortunately, the future in that regard didn't look too shabby. Her mother appeared younger than fifty-four. Donna Casale had maintained the shapely figure that had attracted male interest all her life—leaving her alone and pregnant at twenty-three, but also permitting her to attract a second admiring glance even after age fifty. And years in the retail trade meant she always looked polished and presentable: hair colored, makeup on and smile beaming. Of course, marriage might also have something to do with it these days. Her mother seemed *happy*.

Marisa felt a pang at the contrast to her own circumstances as she let herself be enveloped in a hug. Her mother and Ted had bought a tidy three-bedroom wood-frame house at the time of their wedding. Marisa and Sal had begun talking about buying a home themselves during their brief engagement, but those plans had gone nowhere.

When her mother pulled back from their embrace, she said, "Come on in. You're early, but I couldn't be happier to see you. You're so busy these days!"

Marisa *tried* to keep occupied. She'd plunged back into work after her breakup with Sal, taking on additional roles at Pershing in order to advance her career and keep her mind off depressing thoughts.

Donna closed the front door, and Marisa followed her toward the back of the house.

"I'm so glad you're staying for dinner," Donna said over her shoulder, leading the way down the hall.

"It's a welcome break, Mom, and you spoil me." Still, Marisa wanted to give her mother and Ted their space so they could enjoy their relatively new married life.

"Well, you're just in time to help me assemble the

lasagna," her mother said with a laugh, "so you'll be working for your supper. Ted will be home soon."

When they reached a small but recently remodeled kitchen, Marisa draped her things on a chair, and her mother went to the counter crowded with ingredients and bowls.

Marisa's gaze settled on a framed photo of Donna and Ted on their low-key wedding day. Donna and Ted were all smiles in the picture, her mother clutching a small sprig of flowers that complemented a cream satin tea-length dress. Marisa had been their sole attendant, and one of their witnesses, because Ted had been child-less before his marriage.

Marisa bit back a wistful sigh. She and her mother had always been each other's confidantes—the two of them against the world—but now her mom had some-one else. Marisa couldn't have been happier for her.

It was just… It was just… An image of Cole rose to mind.

What had she been thinking? What had he? He'd kissed her in the storage room last week—and she'd kissed him back. And the memory of that kiss had lin-gered…replayed before she went to sleep at night, while driving to work and during breaks in the school day.

The teenage Cole had nothing on Cole the man. He'd made her come apart in his arms, and it had both shocked and thrilled her. She'd been under the influence at the time, of course. Panic and proximity—mixed with the confession of long-held secrets—had made a heady brew while they'd been locked in together.

Her mother glanced at her, her brows drawing to-gether in concern. "You seem worried. Are you taking care of yourself?"

The question was one that Marisa was used to. Ever since she'd been born a preemie, her mother had worried about her health. She gave a practiced smile. "I'm fine."

"Well, you were a fighter from day one."

Marisa continued smiling, and as she usually did whenever her mother's worries came to the fore, she tried to move the conversation in a different direction. "Serafina found an apartment and is moving out tomorrow."

"I heard."

"I'll have my apartment to myself." Even before her cousin had moved in, she'd hardly felt as if she lived alone. She and Sal had been serious enough that he'd often been at her place or he'd been at hers.

"You should get married."

Marisa bit back another sigh. She hadn't succeeded in steering the talk to safer waters. "I was engaged. It didn't work out."

Ever since her mother had met and then married Ted, she'd viewed marriage in a different light.

"So?" Donna persisted. "He wasn't the right man. You'll meet someone else."

Marisa parted her lips as Cole sprung to mind. *No.* He was her past, not her future, even if he occupied her present. *Get a grip.* "Mom, I know you're still a bit of a newlywed, so you're looking at the world through rose-colored glasses, but—"

Her mother sobered. "Honey, how can you say so? I may be newly married, but I haven't forgotten the years of struggle…"

Donna's amber eyes—so like Marisa's own—clouded, as if recollections of the past were flashing by. Marisa wondered what those memories were. Was her mother recalling the same things she was? The years of juggling bill payments—staying one short step away from having the electricity turned off? The credit card balances that were rolled over because Donna was too proud to ask relatives for a loan?

"I know, Mom," Marisa said quietly. "I was there."

Donna sighed. "And that's part of my guilt."

"What?"

"I didn't shield you enough. Your childhood wasn't as secure as I would have liked it to be."

"You did your best." Wasn't she always telling her students to try their best? "I always felt loved. I graduated from a great school, got a college degree and have a great job."

"Still, I wish you had someone to lean on. I'm not going to be around forever."

"Mom, you're only fifty-four!" In that moment, however, Marisa understood. While she'd worried about her mother, her mother had reciprocated with concern about her.

"I wish I'd left you with siblings," her mother said wistfully.

"You could barely handle me!" Besides, she had cousins. Serafina for one.

"You were a good girl. Mr. Hayes at the Pershing School even came up to me on graduation day to tell me so, and that I'd done a great job raising you."

Marisa smothered a wince and then walked over to the kitchen sink to wash and dry her hands. Naturally, Mr. Hayes had thought she was one of the good guys. She'd ratted out Cole… Marisa had kept her mother in the dark about that part of her life. She hadn't wanted her mother burdened any more than she was.

"How is your job at Pershing, by the way?" Donna asked. "Are the kids taking a lot out of you?"

It wasn't the kids who were responsible for her current turmoil, but a certain six-foot-plus former hockey player. "I'm in charge of the big Pershing Shines Bright benefit in May."

"Ted and I will be there, of course. We want to support you."

"Thanks." Marisa eyed the pasta machine. "You've been busy."

"One of the benefits of having the day off from work. I made the pasta sheets for the lasagna from scratch."

Marisa picked up one of the sheets and set it down in a pan that her mother had already coated with tomato sauce.

"Is the planning going well?" Donna probed.

"It's fine." Marisa shrugged. "Cole Serenghetti of the New England Razors has agreed to headline."

Donna brought her hands together. "Wonderful. He's so popular around here."

Tell me about it. "He's not playing professional hockey anymore. He got hurt."

"Oh yes, I had heard that." Donna frowned. "He was such a good player in high school… Well, until the incident that earned him a suspension."

Marisa kept her expression neutral. "He's running the family construction business these days, though I'm not sure how happy he is about it. His father had a stroke."

Donna's gaze was searching. "You do seem to know a lot about Cole."

"Don't worry, Mom," Marisa responded, setting down more sheets of pasta for the lasagna. "I also knew a lot about Sal before he dumped me. Once burned, twice shy."

"*Dumped* is such an ugly word," Donna said lightly. "*Fortuitously disengaged* is the way I put it for members of my book club."

"Are you doing ad copy for the department store circular these days?" Marisa quipped.

"No, but I did suggest to the book club that we read *Dump the Dude, Buy the Shoes*."

They shared a laugh before Marisa said, "You did not!"

Actually she thought the title might not be a bad one for the autobiography of her mother's life.

"No, I was joking. But I did tell everyone that I got promoted to buyer for housewares." Donna spooned a thin layer of ricotta cheese mixture on top of the layer of pasta that Marisa had created.

"They must have been thrilled for you." Before Marisa could say any more, she heard her cell phone buzz. Wiping her hands on a dish towel, she walked over to get the phone out of her handbag. When she saw the message on the screen, her heart began to pound.

Told Dobson our meeting cut short b/c I had other business. Let's reschedule. Dinner Friday @6. LMK.

"Is everything okay?" Donna asked, studying her.

"Speak of the devil," Marisa said, trying for some lame humor. "No, not Sal. The other devil. Cole Serenghetti."

Donna's eyebrows rose. "He's texting you? So you do know each other well!"

"First time. He must have a record of my cell number—" she paused to consider for a moment, thinking back "—because I had to call him to discuss something related to the fund-raiser and new gym." She was *not* going to mention to her mother that she'd visited Cole's offices. Because that might lead to mention of the incident in the storage room. And she was *so* not discussing that mishap. Especially with her mother. Even if she was thirty-three and an adult.

"Well?"

"He's invited me to dinner." As her mother's eyebrows shot higher, she added, "A business dinner."

She should go. She was grateful that he'd covered for her with Mr. Dobson. She was also relieved he was willing to keep dealing with her about the fund-raiser and construction project. It wouldn't look good if Cole announced he needed a different contact person at Pershing. And she had twenty questions about what he had to say—who wouldn't?

Dinner? Really?

Still, it wasn't as if they were having an assignation. As she'd told her mother, it was a business meeting. Pure business. The kiss last time notwithstanding. A blip on the radar never, ever to be repeated.

And now that Cole had agreed to the fund-raiser, she'd begun flirting with another idea—that is, until the storage room incident…

Donna continued to regard her. "Honey, trust me, I'm acquainted with the attractiveness of professional athletes."

Marisa knew they were no longer talking only about Cole. They'd both been burned long ago by another man chasing sports fame, except he'd been a baseball player. "This is purely business, believe me."

Marisa wished she could wholeheartedly believe it herself. So she and Cole had shared a kiss. Given the unusual circumstances—her panic and his need to reassure and, uh, comfort—they had an excuse. One that her mother didn't need to hear.

As her mother searched her expression, Marisa stuck to her best Girl Scout face and walked back to the kitchen counter.

Finally, seemingly satisfied—or not—Donna sighed. "We should find time to write that dude book together. Meanwhile, let's finish this lasagna, and I'll open a bottle of wine."

"What's this about, Cole?"

"Dinner. What else?" He looked bemusedly at the woman sitting to his left—the one who had bedeviled more of his nights and days than he cared to count. He'd chosen Welsdale's chicest restaurant, Bayart's on Creek Road, and she'd proposed meeting him there—much to his chagrin. He'd gone along with her suggestion, even though he saw through it as the defensive move it was, because he knew he was still treading on fragile ground with Marisa. He'd ordered a bottle of Merlot, and the waiter had already poured their wine.

Tonight she was in a geometric-print wrap dress that left no curve untouched. *My God, the woman is set on torturing me.*

"I mean the subtext."

He raised his gaze to her eyes. "Subtext? You were always a stellar student in English."

"And you spent your time in the last row, goofing around."

"Charlotte Brontë wasn't my thing."

"She was about the only female who wasn't."

"She was dead."

"Don't let that stop you."

He grinned. "That's what I discovered I liked about you, Danieli. You're able to serve it up straight when you want to. Back then, and now."

"I'm a teacher. It's a survival skill."

"I liked you better than you think, you know."

"Well, that's something, I suppose. Right up there with being someone's sixth favorite teacher."

He laughed because he liked this more uninhibited Marisa—one who felt free to speak her mind. "Still feeling the effect of your confession last time? You're letting it rip. It's—" he let his voice dip "—enticing."

She got an adorable little pucker in her brow and toyed with the stem of her wineglass. "It wasn't intended to be, but why am I not surprised you took it that way?"

"I really did like you," he insisted.

"You're just saying that," she demurred.

"Are you ready to talk about what happened in the storage room?" It was safer than focusing on the wineglass in her hand and imagining her fingers on him.

They could have been on a date, from outward appearances, because Bayart's candlelit interior invited intimacy. In keeping with the restaurant's formality, Cole was still in the navy suit that he'd worn to the office. And Marisa was probably expecting tonight to be all business…

"Wow, you're direct." Marisa blew out a breath. "Isn't it obvious? We're destined for close encounters in small spaces."

He smiled at her attempt at humor and deflection. "Try again." When she still said nothing, he continued,

"I'll go first. I wonder what you saw in me while we were in high school. I was a jock and a jerk."

She joined him in smiling, and it was like the sun coming out. "That's an easy one. I admired you. You were willing to take risks. On the ice, you took chances in order to win. And off the ice, you skated on the edge with your pranks. I was meek, and you were confident. I was quiet, and you were popular."

"I was a jerk, and you weren't."

She blinked, and the curve of her lips wobbled.

"Fat lot of good it did me, too. I ultimately wound up crashing and burning, on the ice and off." It was his offer of a mea culpa—accepting guilt and responsibility. Fifteen years ago she'd called a halt to his pranks. And if he'd been a jerk in the aftermath, it had been for nothing. He'd still gotten a professional career on the ice, and when it had ended, it had had nothing to do with Marisa.

"You know what they say. Better to have tried and failed than never to have tried at all…"

"You've never taken risks?" he probed.

"Well, I did recruit you for the Pershing benefit. I guess you bring out the daredevil in me."

"Yeah," he drawled. "The same way I tempted you to test out the theater department's prop during senior year."

Marisa looked embarrassed.

Before he could say more, the waiter came up to take their order. Marisa waffled on what to have, but settled on the Cobb salad.

"You can't choose a salad," Cole said with dry humor. "It's a sin in a place like this."

"It's not," she responded lightly. "I'm sure everything is delicious here."

Including her. He could tell she'd contemplated ordering a richer entrée, and he wanted to say he appreciated every inch of her lush curves, but he let it go. Maybe a salad was Marisa's go-to choice on a date—not that she thought of this as a date, but certainly dinner with a man. *Him.*

When the waiter had departed, the conversation turned to casual topics, but Cole was determined to shift gears back to what they had been discussing.

At a lull, he said, "It must have given you some satisfaction to see me taken down a peg or two in high school. After all, we did have sex, and then I avoided you."

"It hurt."

"I wasn't prepared to deal with what had happened between us. You were a virgin, and you caught me off guard. I might not have hurt you when we fumbled our way through sex, but I did in other ways."

She lowered her lashes. "We were both young and stupid."

"Teenagers make mistakes," he concurred.

She toyed some more with the wineglass, making him crazy. "It must have been an unwelcome surprise when we were first paired up to make a PowerPoint presentation in economics class."

"Not unwelcome," he replied, shifting. "You were an unknown quantity."

"A nonentity at school, especially among the jocks."

He shook his head. "Sweet pea, you may be a teacher, but you still have no idea how most teenage boys think. The only reason the jocks didn't know how big your breasts were is because you were always hiding them behind a bunch of books."

She stared at him. "You were looking at my chest?"

He smiled wolfishly. "On the sly. And I wasn't just looking. Do you think that whenever I brushed by you during our study sessions it was an accident?"

Her eyes widened, and her hand fell away from the wineglass.

"Definitely a C cup."

"I'm not a simple bra size!"

He reached out and covered her hand on the table, smoothing his thumb over the back of her palm. *Anything to avoid further arousal by her fingertips on a damn glass.* "You're right. I got to know the person beyond the teenage boy's fantasy, and you scared the hell out of me."

"I did?"

The look in her eyes was so earnest, it was all he could do not to lean in and capture her lips.

Instead, he nodded. "I started out a little intrigued and a whole lot bored when I was assigned as your partner in economics. But then I got near you, and the hormones kicked in. A few study sessions staring into your eyes, and I was toast. You were nice, smart and interesting."

"I had a crush on you even before we were paired up to do an assignment," she admitted. "All it took was some casual contact, and I was hooked."

"I didn't need a whole lot of convincing to ditch the books in favor of getting closer to you." They had progressed from kissing to more the next time they were together. And then after a few encounters, they'd really gotten intimate…

"But I bet I'm the first girl who got you involved with a theater department prop."

"I'll never forget that velvet sofa." As a scholarship student, Marisa had had a part-time job helping the custodial department clean the school, so she'd had access to a very convenient set of keys.

"They still have it."

He raised his brows. "Then you'll have to give me a tour when I'm at the school."

She parted her lips, but didn't take the bait, so he slid back his hand.

He angled his head, contemplating her. "You wanted me as badly as I wanted you, so I was surprised when it turned out to be your first time. Why did you do it?"

She shrugged. "I was hungry for affection and attention. I wanted to fit in."

"You were a virgin. You'd gotten under my skin and seen beyond the prankster and the jock. It was too heavy for me, so I did the only logical thing for an eighteen-year-old guy. I avoided you."

"Right, I recall," she said drily.

"You were the first woman to proposition me."

"But not the last."

"For professional athletes, propositioning usually goes with the territory."

"So women like Vicki the Vixen are always throwing themselves at you in bars?"

He bit back a smile at the moniker he was sure Vicki wouldn't appreciate. "I'm not a hockey player anymore. These days I'm a CEO…and Pershing School's knight in shining armor."

The waiter arrived with their food, and they dropped their conversation while plates were set before them and they exchanged polite niceties with their server. Then Marisa tucked daintily into her Cobb salad while Cole mentally shrugged and dug into his filet mignon and potatoes au gratin.

After several moments Marisa took a sip of her wine. "You called yourself Pershing's knight in shining armor." She paused. "And I, uh, have another way for you to shine."

He searched her face, and she cleared her throat.

"I have students who would enjoy a field trip to the Razors' arena as part of Career Week."

He sat back in his chair, his lips twisting with amusement. "It's one request after another with you."

"Since you seem to be more approachable these days, I figured I had nothing to lose."

"I don't come cheap."

"I know. Last time you got a construction contract out of the bargain."

He inclined his head in acknowledgment. Ever since their encounter in the storage room, he'd thought about how it would feel to cup her face in his hands again and thread his fingers in her hair. He'd bet her long curly locks fanned across his pillow would be spectacular—and erotic.

"So what's it going to be this time?" she asked.

He could think of a lot of things he'd like to bargain for. "An answer to a question. I'm curious."

She looked surprised and then wary. "That's it?"

He felt a smile tug at his lips. "You haven't heard the question yet."

She shifted in her seat. "Okay…"

"Why Sal? There are a lot of seemingly reliable, boring guys out there."

She stared at him a moment, eyes wide, and then took a deep breath. "Timing."

"I can appreciate the importance. Timing is everything, on the ice and off."

"Yes, and ours has never been great."

He had to agree with her there. "And Sal's was?"

"It was part of it."

"Which part?"

"My mother had just gotten married…"

"And Sal was available when you were vulnerable?"

"Something like that," she admitted.

"I can understand family responsibility, Marisa. Your mother getting married set you free and maybe even adrift."

She looked surprised by his insight. Hell, he was surprised himself. Where had that bit of pop psychology come from? Too much latent baggage from his own family floating to the surface?

Marisa wet her lips. "I guess I didn't want my mother to worry about me anymore once she was married."

"So Sal had it on timing?" *As opposed to a former hockey player?*

"He can also be quite charming when he wants to be."

"So is a used car salesman," Cole quipped. "So Sal laid on the charm…?"

"He was there, and the type I was looking for."

Cole quirked his lips. "You have a type? I thought your type was high school prankster."

She shook her head. "My goal was to marry someone not like my father."

"You knew him?" He didn't recall Marisa ever men-

tioning her father in high school except to say he'd died
a long time ago.

"No, he passed away before I was born. But I'd always thought my parents had meant to get married. In my twenties, I found out that wasn't the case…"

Cole said nothing, waiting for her to go on.

"My mother finally revealed my father had broken up with her even before he died in a car accident. He was out of the picture before she gave birth."

"So your father's side of the family was never involved in your life?"

Marisa nodded. "My father's only surviving relative was my grandfather, who lived on the West Coast. As for my father, he was pursuing a minor league baseball career, and a wife and baby didn't fit with his plans. He had big dreams and wanderlust."

"So you believed Sal was the guy for you because he wasn't bitten by the same bug."

"I thought he was the right man. I was wrong."

Cole suddenly understood. Marisa had thought Sal would never leave her. He wasn't a professional athlete whose career came first. In other words, Sal was unlike her father…and unlike Cole, who'd left Welsdale at the first opportunity for hockey.

Marisa had discovered the truth about her father long after she'd finished high school at Pershing. So if Cole's reaction after missing out on a potential hockey championship at Pershing hadn't soured her on athletes, then the truth she learned about her father in her twenties certainly would have.

As Marisa steered the conversation back to scheduling a student field trip to the Razors' arena, as well as setting up another time for her to review Serenghetti

Construction's old architectural plans, Cole realized one thing.

He'd had his chance with Marisa at eighteen, but these days she was looking for something—someone—different.

Six

Marisa had never been inside the New England Razors arena, which was located outside Springfield, Massachusetts. The closeness to the state border allowed the team to attract a sizable crowd from nearby Connecticut as well as from their home base, Massachusetts.

Marisa had just never counted herself among those fans. She'd always felt that going to a game would be a painful blast from the past where Cole was concerned. The Razors' games were televised, but she could handle Cole Serenghetti's power over her memories—sort of—when it was limited to a glimpse of a screen in a restaurant or other public place.

Right now, however, she was getting the full Cole Serenghetti effect as he stood a few feet away addressing a group of Pershing high school students. He was dressed in faded blue jeans and a long-sleeved black tee. His clothing was casual, but no less potent on her senses. She was sensitive to his every move, and was having a hard time denying what it was: sexual awareness.

"Look," Cole said to the kids arrayed before him in a semicircle inside the front entrance, "since it's a Saturday and this is a half-day field trip, we'll do a tour of the arena first and then some ice-skating. How does that sound?"

Some kids smiled, and others nodded their heads.

"And how many of you want to be professional hockey players?"

A few hands shot up. Marisa was glad to see those of three girls among them. Pershing fielded both boys' and girls' hockey teams, but the girls tended to drop out at a higher rate than the boys once they hit high school.

One of the students raised his hand. "Does your injury still bother you?"

Marisa sucked in a breath.

"It's important to wear protective equipment," Cole said. "Injuries do happen, but they're unusual, especially the serious ones."

The kids remained silent, as if they expected him to go on.

"In my case, I tore up my knee twice. I had surgery and therapy both times. After the second, I could walk without a problem, but playing professional hockey wasn't in the cards." Cole's tone was even and matter-of-fact, and he betrayed no hint that the subject was a touchy one for him. "I was past thirty, and I'd already had several great seasons with the New England Razors. I had another career calling me."

"So now you do construction?" a student piped up from the back row.

Cole gave a self-deprecating laugh. "Yup. But as CEO, I spend more time in the office than on a job site. I make sure we stay within our budget and that resources are allocated correctly among projects." He cast Marisa a sidelong look. "I also go out and drum up more business."

Marisa felt heat flood her cheeks even though she was the only one who could guess what Cole was alluding to.

A few days ago she and Cole had finally had their intended meeting at his offices to go over architectural plans for past projects. When she'd shown up this time, Cole had had the plans ready for review in a conference room. She must have appeared relieved that she wouldn't have to step back inside Serenghetti Construction's storage room, because Cole had shot her an amused and knowing look. Still, she'd gotten enough information to go back to Mr. Dobson with no surprises but some valuable input.

Fortunately, they hadn't had the opportunity to discuss their encounter in the storage room. Every time Cole had looked as if he was about to bring it up, they'd been interrupted by a phone call or by an employee with a question.

Cole scanned the small crowd assembled before him. "Today I'm going to show you career fields connected to hockey that you might not have thought of. Sure there are the players on the ice that everyone sees during the game. Their names make the news. But behind them is a whole other team of people who make professional hockey what it is."

"Like who?" a couple of kids asked, speaking over each other.

"Well, I'm going to take you to the broadcast booth, in case anyone is interested in sports journalism. We'll walk through the management offices to talk to marketing. And then we'll go down to the locker rooms, where the sports medicine people do their stuff. Sound good?"

The kids nodded.

"I'll stop before I show you the construction stuff," Cole quipped.

"Is that how you stayed involved with your old sport?" a ninth grader asked.

"Yup." Cole flashed a smile. "We repaved the ground outside the arena."

From her position a little removed from the crowd, Marisa sighed because Cole had a natural ability to connect with kids. He was effortlessly cool, and she was… not. Some things never changed.

Cole winked at her, shaking her out of her musings. "And if you're all good, there might also be an appearance by Jordan Serenghetti—"

The kids let out whoops.

"—who is having a great season with the Razors. But more important, in my opinion, he's having an even better life as my younger brother."

Everyone laughed.

Marisa thought Jordan would dispute Cole's assessment if he were there.

After Cole gave the kids a tour of the parts of the arena that he had referred to, he led the group to the ice rink.

As everyone laced up their skates, Marisa overheard a couple of the kids talking about her with Cole. When they mentioned to him that she was a fantastic cook, she felt heat rush to her face.

She hung back and skated onto the ice after everyone else. She was wearing tights and a tunic-length sweater so her movements weren't restricted, but she hadn't been on skates in a long time. She became aware of Cole watching her, hands in pockets, as the others glided around.

"I wasn't sure what to expect," he said.

She continued to skate at a leisurely pace, now only a few feet away from him. "I've had ice-skating lessons."

He arched a brow.

"It's New England. Everyone assumes you know how to stay upright on the ice."

To underscore her words, she did several swizzles, her legs swerving in and out.

"Looks like you did more than learn how to stay upright," Cole commented. "Where did you learn?"

"At the rec center outside Welsdale," she admitted, slowing. "It opened when we were kids, and they gave free lessons."

"I know. My father built it."

She stared at him and then gave an unsurprised laugh. "I should have guessed."

She thought a moment, concentrated and then gaining speed, did a scratch spin. Glancing back at Cole, now meters away, she shrugged and added, "I picked up a few moves."

She wasn't sure how many moves she could still do, but it seemed that as with riding a bike, some skills she'd never lose.

"So when did you change course from budding skating star to top-notch teacher?" Cole asked as he skated toward her.

She shrugged again. "We didn't have the money for me to pursue the sport seriously. It would have meant lessons, costumes and travel expenses. When I was accepted to Pershing, I had to concentrate on getting good grades in order to keep my scholarship."

She tensed as soon as the word *scholarship* was out of her mouth because they were close to the big bugaboo topic between them. Still, the truth was that Cole had gotten to play in the NHL while she'd received her coveted scholarship and moved on to teaching—a nice, stable profession rather than glitz and glory. He'd been able to afford his dreams while she hadn't.

"I was signed up for figure skating and ice dancing lessons as a kid—"

She laughed because she couldn't envision Cole doing the waltz—on the ice or off. He was too big…too male.

"—but they didn't take," he finished drily.

She bit the inside of her cheek, trying to school her expression. She was a lot better at keeping a straight face in the classroom.

"My mother was determined to make her sons into little gentlemen."

Marisa willed herself to appear earnest. *Instead Mrs. Serenghetti had gotten a bunch of pranksters.*

"You think this is funny."

She nodded, not trusting herself to speak.

"Here, I'll demonstrate," he said, approaching. "I remember a thing or two."

She blinked. "What?"

"We're here to show these kids careers related to hockey."

"Like ice dancing? I thought that branching out usually went the other way."

"Like if you sucked at ice dancing as a kid, you took up hockey instead?"

She raised her eyebrows.

"So now I'm a failed figure skater? Someone who couldn't hack it?" He rubbed his chin. "I have something to prove."

She didn't like the sound of that. But before she could respond, he reached for her hand and then slid his other around her waist, so that they were facing each other in dance position.

"What are you doing?" she asked in a high voice, caught between surprise and breathlessness at his nearness.

"Like I said, I have something to prove. I hope you remember your figure skating moves, sweet pea."

The arm around her was a band of pure muscle. He worked out, and it showed. The power he exuded made her nervous, so she didn't raise her gaze above his mouth—though *that* had potency enough to wreak havoc on her heart.

She and Cole skated over the ice, doing a fair facsimile of dancing together. His hands on her were warm imprints, heating her against the cold of the ice.

When she stole a peek at him, she quickly concluded he was still devastatingly gorgeous. His hair was thick and ruffled, inviting a woman to run her fingers through it. His jaw was firm and square but shadowed, promising a hint of roughness. His lips were firm but sensual. And the scar—oh, the scar. The one on his cheek gave character and invited tenderness. He was a catalog of sexy contrasts—a magnet for women in a much blunter way than Jordan. She lowered her lashes. *But not for me*.

"Are you ready for a throw jump?"

Her gaze shot to his. "What?" She sounded like a parrot but she couldn't have heard him right. "I thought we were just dancing! What about your knee?"

He shrugged. "It couldn't take repeated hits from a defenseman who weighs over two hundred pounds, but I'm guessing you don't weigh nearly as much."

"I'm not telling you how much I weigh!"

"Naturally." Cole's eyes crinkled. "Here we go, Ice Princess. Think you can land a throw waltz jump?"

In the next moment they were spinning around and Cole was lifting her off the ice.

"Ready?" he murmured.

She felt herself moving through the air. It was a gentle throw, so she didn't go very high or far. She brought down the toe of her right foot and landed her blade before extending her left leg back.

Cole grinned, and the kids around them on the ice laughed and clapped while a few chortled.

"A one-footed landing," Cole said, skating toward her. "I'm impressed. You've still got game, sweet pea."

She laughed. "Still, can you see me competing in the Olympics?" she asked, gesturing at her ample chest. "I'd have had to bind myself."

Cole gave her a half-lidded look as he stopped in front of her. "Now that would be a shame."

She'd walked into that one. Students glided by around them, and there were a few gasps as Jordan appeared. This was hardly the place for Cole and her to be having a sexually tinged moment.

"Relax," Cole said in a low voice. "Nobody is paying attention to us anymore."

Easy for you to say. She tingled with the urge to touch him again. "Cole Serenghetti, too cool for school."

"If you were the teacher, I'd have had my butt glued to my seat in the front row."

"You say that now," she teased, even as his nearness continued to affect her like a drug.

"I was a callow teenager who couldn't appreciate what you were going through."

"Callow?" she queried, still trying to keep it light. "Are you trying to impress the teacher with your vocabulary?"

He bent his head until his lips were inches from hers. "How am I doing?"

Oh wow. "Great," she said a bit breathlessly. "Keep at it, and you might even get an A."

It was the pep talk that she usually gave her students. *Keep trying, work hard and the reward will come...* The moral of her own life story, really. Well, except for her *love* life...

Cole's eyes gleamed as he straightened and murmured, "I've never cared about grades."

She didn't want to ask what he did care about. She'd guess his currency of choice was kisses—and more... Troublingly, she could seriously envision getting tangled up with Cole again even though she should know better...

Cole swiveled on his bar stool and looked at the entrance again.

This time he was finally rewarded with the sight of Marisa coming toward him. She was wearing jeans—

ones that hugged her curves—and a mint-colored sweater. She had on light makeup, but it was a toss-up whether her curls or her chest was bouncier.

Cole felt his groin tighten.

He hadn't been sure she would show. His text had been vague.

Meet me at the Puck & Shoot. I have a plan u need to hear.

Ever since he'd upheld his end of the bargain by giving her students a tour of the Razors' arena, he'd been desperate to come up with another excuse to see her.

She stopped in front of him. "I heard women proposition you in bars these days."

"Care to make one?"

"How about a drink instead?"

"That's a start." He stood, closing the distance between them even further. "What'll you have?"

"A light beer."

Cole fought a smile. "Lightweight, are you?"

"Only in bars, not in the boxing ring."

"Yeah, I know." At the gym, she could pack a wallop in a simple dress that brought grown men to a standstill. But she wasn't too shabby in bars, either. She could still make him stand up and take notice. Without the baggage of her seeming betrayal in high school, he could acknowledge without reservation what a beautiful woman she was.

He signaled the bartender and placed an order.

She glanced around, as if uncertain. "This is my first visit to the Puck & Shoot."

"I thought you said this is where you got a tip about how to run me to ground at Jimmy's Boxing Gym."

"I wouldn't call it *running to ground*," she said pertly. "You were still standing when I left the boxing ring. Also, I didn't say I got the tip personally. My cousin Serafina has been moonlighting as a waitress here. She overheard some of the Razors talking."

"Like those at the other end of the bar?" Cole indicated with his chin. "The ones wondering what the status of our relationship is?"

Marisa tossed a glance over her shoulder. "Probably, but we don't have a relationship with a status."

He brought his finger to his lips. "Shh, don't tell. I like having them wonder why a gorgeous woman passed them over and made a beeline in my direction instead."

"You asked me to come here!"

He laughed at her with his eyes. "They don't know that, sweet pea." He reached out to smooth a strand of hair away from her face and remembered all over again how soft her skin was.

His body tightened another notch and she stilled, like a deer in headlights.

"I don't think Serafina likes the Razors very much…"

He settled his gaze on her mouth. "They can be a randy bunch."

"You included?"

"I'll let you be the judge," he responded lazily.

He wanted her. *Right now.* He'd dreamed about her again last night, and it had been his hottest fantasy ever.

"Jordan isn't the only joker in the family."

He handed her the beer that had just been set down on the bar and then watched as Marisa placed her lips on the bottle's long neck and took a swill. The woman was killing him with her sexual tone deafness.

"So where's Serafina?" he asked.

Marisa lowered the bottle. "She isn't working to-night. Wednesday isn't on her regular schedule, and she's about to quit for a better position."

"If this had been her shift, would you have met me here?"

"Maybe."

He smiled. "Or maybe not."

He took it as a good sign that Marisa wanted to keep their meetings on the down-low. It meant she cared what people thought about the two of them. *Like maybe there was something going on.* Which there was, whether Marisa would admit it or not. Still, she was skittish about the sexual attraction that still existed between them, and he needed to proceed carefully.

They were both adults, and he was itching to explore what had gotten cut short in high school. As long as he was indefinitely parked in Welsdale, there was no rea-son not to enjoy himself...

He let his gaze sweep over her. Besides the jeans and sweater, she wore black high-heeled Mary-Janes that showed off her shapely legs. She'd subverted the most schoolmarmish of shoes and made them sexy and hot...

Marisa raised her eyebrows as if she'd read his thoughts. "Why did you want to meet?"

Because he wasn't ready to share his sexy thoughts, he leaned against the bar stool behind him and gestured to the empty one next to him. "Have a seat."

"Thank you, but I'm fine."

Definitely skittish. Even leaning back, he still had a height advantage on her, but he had to admire her unwillingness to give an additional inch. Time to show some of his cards. "I noticed some of the kids on the field trip were interested in hockey. I'd like to give them a few pointers."

His offer, of course, was a pretext for getting her to meet with him again.

Marisa took her time answering, her face reflecting flitting emotions until it settled into an expression of determination. "I don't just want you to give them a few pointers. I want you to run a hockey clinic."

Right back at you. He'd underestimated her. "That's a tall order. Giving a few pointers is one thing, and setting up a sports clinic is another. Let me clarify in case you don't understand—"

"Never having been a jock."

"—but training sessions involve drawing up practice plans and small area games—"

"So the kids will have others to play against."

"—and it's a big investment of time."

"You're up to the challenge," she ended encouragingly.

What he was up for was getting her into bed. "I'll tell you what. I'll start with informal coaching for a small group."

She nodded and smiled. "Now that that's settled, let's discuss the remarks you'll be giving at the fund-raiser."

The woman didn't miss a beat. But now it was his turn to hit the puck back at her. "If you search online, you'll come up with my past speeches. My talk to the sports group in Boston on working hard and realizing your dreams. My humorous anecdotes about my rookie year in the NHL—"

"You'll want to say something flattering about the Pershing School." She looked earnest as she said it.

"And my time there?" he queried. "How do I work in my suspension—" he leaned forward confidentially "—or the episode on the theater department's casting couch?"

She shifted. "I thought we'd established I didn't land you a suspension out of retaliation."

"No, but I still think of it as a...highlight of my high school career. How do I discuss my time at Pershing without mentioning it?"

"Stick to sports and academics," she sidestepped. "And it wasn't a casting couch. You're not a Hollywood starlet who had to put out for the sake of her career."

He grinned. "Yeah, but you were definitely auditioning me for the role of study buddy with benefits. How did I do?"

"Could have been better," she harrumphed.

"I am now, sweet pea. Don't you want to find out how much better?" He liked teasing her, and what's more, he couldn't help it.

Her gaze skittered away from his and then stopped in the distance, her eyes widening.

She looked back at him and flushed.

Before he could react, she leaned forward, cupped his face with both her hands and pressed her lips to his.

What the...? It was Cole's last thought before he went motionless.

Her lips felt soft and full, and she tasted sweet. Her floral scent wafted to him. He was surprised by the fact that she'd made the first move, but he was more than happy to oblige...

He parted his lips and pulled her forward.

She slipped into the gap between his legs, her arms encircling his neck.

He caressed her lips with his and then deepened the kiss. He stroked her tongue, tangling with her and swallowing her moan.

The sounds of the bar receded, and he brought a laser focus to the woman in his arms. He silently urged Marisa even closer so that her breasts pressed into him.

Come on. More...

"Talk about a surprise."

The words sounded from behind him, and Marisa pulled away.

Cole caught her startled, guilty look before he turned and straightened, and saw Sal Piazza's too-jovial expression. Vicki clung to Sal's arm, her face betraying shock.

Glancing at Marisa, Cole suddenly understood everything. He settled his face into a bland expression and forced himself back from their heated kiss.

Sal held out his hand. "I didn't expect to see you here, Cole."

"Piazza," he acknowledged.

Vicki's expression subsided from shock to surprise.

Sal dropped his hand as his gaze moved from Marisa to Cole. "You two are together."

It was a simple statement, but there was a wealth of curiosity behind it.

Cole felt Marisa go tense beside him and knew there was only one thing to do. He slid an arm around her waist before responding, "Yup. Not many people know."

Actually, it had been a party of two until seconds ago. And even then, *he* hadn't been sure what was up. That kiss had come out of nowhere and packed a punch even bigger than the one in the storage room.

Sal cleared his throat. "Marisa and I haven't been in touch since the break—"

"Lots of things can happen around a breakup." Cole made it a flat statement—and deliberately left the implication that he and Marisa had started getting acquainted at the same time that she and Sal had broken up.

Sal looked affronted, and Cole tightened his arm around Marisa as she shifted.

Sal twisted his lips in a sardonic smile. "Well, I—"

"Congratulations, I suppose," Vicki piped in with an edge to her voice.

Marisa smiled at the other woman. "Thanks, but we really haven't told many people about our relationship yet."

Cole kept his bland expression. Oh yeah, Marisa was with him. After this was over, though, he'd be quizzing her about their supposed liaison, including that kiss... Had she only planted one on him because she'd spotted Sal and Vicki?

Sal gave a forced laugh. "I guess a little partner swapping is going on."

Cole fixed him with a hard look.

Glancing at Marisa, Vicki narrowed her eyes and thrust her chin forward. "Be careful, sweetie. He's not one to commit."

"Which one?" Marisa quipped.

As Vicki's mouth dropped open, Cole found himself caught between laughing and wincing. They were a train wreck waiting to happen—or a hockey brawl.

"We're here for a corner booth and some dinner," Sal said grimly, his gaze moving between Marisa and Cole, "so we'll cede the bar to you two. Nice running into you."

Without a backward glance, Sal and Vicki headed toward the rear room of the crowded bar.

Cole figured that with any luck, he wouldn't catch a glimpse of the other couple again, which left Marisa and him to their own private reckoning...

Marisa slipped away from the arm around her waist, and her gaze collided with his.

"I'd hate to meet you in the ring," he remarked drily.

She sighed. "You already have."

"Yeah," he said with a touch of humor, "but that time Jordan was there to protect me."

Marisa compressed her lips.

"Well, this is an interesting turn of events," he drawled.

She seemed flustered and shrugged. "Who knew that Sal would show up with Vicki?"

"Since this is a sports bar, and he's a sports agent, not so far-fetched. Besides, it's not what I'm talking about, hot lips."

"I like *sweet pea* better," she responded distractedly. "Anyway, it seemed like a good idea at the time."

"I doubt thinking entered into it. Reacting is more like it."

"Well, making it seem as if we were involved was an easy shortcut answer to what we were doing in a bar together."

"How about the truth, instead?"

"Not nearly as satisfying."

"You got me there," he conceded.

They continued to stare at each other. She was inches away, emanating a palpable feminine energy.

"You know they're going to tell people," he remarked. "The news is too good not to share."

She looked worried. "I know."

He tilted his head, contemplating her.

"We'll have to let people wonder, and the gossip will fizzle out in time."

He shook his head. "Not nearly as satisfying."

She gazed at him quizzically. "As what?"

"As making it seem as if we really are a couple."

"What?"

Her voice came out as a high-pitched squeak, and he had to smile.

"Now that the cat is out of the bag, we'll need to keep up the ruse for a while in order to keep the fallout from hurting both our reputations."

"But I just explained it'll fizz—"

"Not fast enough. People are going to conclude we were trying to get back at our exes."

She looked stung, but then her expression became resolute. "All right, but we keep up the charade only until the fund-raiser. That should be enough time for this to pass out of public conversation."

He thought she was deluding herself about that last part, but he let it go. "Sal must really mean something for you to have pulled that stunt."

He wasn't jealous, just curious, he told himself.

She shook her head. "No, it's more about being dumped for someone who looked like a better bet."

"Vicki?"

"I can't believe you dated her," she huffed.

"Hey, you're the one who went so far as to get engaged—" he jerked his thumb to indicate the back of the bar "—to *that.*"

"The correct pronoun is *him. To him,*" she responded.

"Maybe for school, but not in hockey."

"Why do men—athletes—date women like Vicki?"

He flashed his teeth. "Because we can."

"Sal thinks he can, too."

He picked up his beer bottle and saluted her with it before taking a swig. "After that kiss, I'd say our relationship now qualifies as having a *status*."

Her eyes widened as the truth of his words sank in.

She was an intriguing mix, with the power to blindside him more than any offensive player on the ice. Back in high school and now.

And things were only going to get more interesting since she'd just handed him a plum excuse for continuing to see her...

Seven

He was in heaven.

A beautiful woman had just opened the door to her apartment. And delicious aromas wafted toward him.

Marisa, however, looked shocked to see him.

"What are you doing here?" she demanded.

She was wearing a white tee and a red-and-black apron with an abundance of frills. She had bare legs, and a ridiculous pair of mule slippers with feathers on them showed off her red pedicure.

His body tightened.

Hey, if she wanted to role-play, he was all for it. She could be a sexy domestic goddess, and he could be the guy who knocked on the door and…obliged her.

She was still staring at him. Devoid of any makeup, she looked fresh-faced and casual.

"What are you doing here?" she asked again.

He thought fast. "Is that any way to greet your newest—" What was the status of their relationship anyway? "Love interest?"

"We both know it isn't real!"

"It's real," he countered, "but temporary."

She looked unconvinced.

Ever since their encounter at the Puck & Shoot late last week, he'd been searching for another way to see her again. He'd decided the direct approach was the only and best option this time.

"People will expect me to drop in on my girlfriend." He arched an eyebrow and added pointedly, "And at least know what her place looks like."

She leaned against the door. "Our relationship isn't genuine."

"Everyone seems to think it is."

"We're the only two people that matter."

"How real did that kiss in the bar feel to you?" He wasn't sure how far the news had traveled—he hadn't gotten any inquisitive phone calls from his family *yet*— but sooner or later there was bound to be gossip. Sal and Vicki weren't the only witnesses to the kiss at the Puck & Shoot.

Marisa's brows drew together. "Shouldn't you be insulted that I used you for an ulterior motive?"

He shrugged. "I don't feel objectified. If a beautiful woman wants to jump my bones, she'll get no argument from me."

She tilted her head. "Why am I not surprised you wouldn't put up a fight?"

He gave a lazy smile, but he didn't miss the quick once-over she gave him from under lowered lashes. Her gaze lingered on the faded jeans he wore under a rust-colored tee and light jacket. Apparently, he wasn't the only one fascinated by clothing's ability to hide—and reveal.

"You're persistent."

"Is it working?"

Sighing, she stepped aside, and he made it over the threshold.

She locked the door behind him, and then touched her hair, which was pulled willy-nilly into a messy knot at the back of her head. Strands escaped, including one that trailed along her nape.

He wanted to loosen the band that prevented her riotous curls from cascading down. There was a large mirror in a yellow scroll frame behind Marisa, so he got a great 360-degree view of her. Underneath the apron, she was wearing a pair of black exercise shorts that hugged a well-rounded rear end.

He needed divine assistance. "You look like you worked out or are about to."

He'd gone out on an early-morning run, but Marisa seemed to prefer to exercise after her school day was finished.

She looked uncomfortable. "I'm trying to get in shape."

She had a fabulous body as far as he was concerned. Her shape was more than fine. Still, if she wanted to exercise, he knew how they could get a workout in bed…

She wet her lips and turned. "Come on in."

He followed her from the foyer and down the hallway, deeper into the apartment.

"It's a prewar building, so this condo has a traditional layout. No open floor plan, like those renovated old factory buildings that you might be used to."

"Something smells delicious." *And someone looked delectable, too.* It was only four-thirty, but maybe Marisa liked to eat early. There was a living room off the hall, done in a flower motif—from plum-colored drapes to a damask armchair covered by a rose throw.

"Parent-teacher conferences are tomorrow night. The school usually has catered fare for the staff, but I got a request to bring my eggplant parmigiana."

They passed two bedrooms, but only the second looked occupied. It had aqua walls offset by white wicker furniture and a white counterpane. There was a mirrored dresser, and a vanity framed by floor-length window treatments.

At the end of the hall, they reached a bright but dated kitchen. The aromas stimulated his taste buds. If she'd been set on seducing him, she couldn't have planned it better.

"I didn't know you were going to show up," she said, as if addressing his private thoughts. "I was mixing the ingredients for cupcakes."

He was going down…but he adopted a solemn expression. "I understand. You're cooking for others."

She gave him a sidelong look. "Well, I did make an extra pan of the eggplant parmigiana to keep around. Would you like some? I just removed it from the oven."

"I'd love some," he said with heartfelt fervor.

Eggplant parmigiana was one of his favorite dishes, but ever since he'd moved out of his parents' house, he didn't often get a home-cooked meal. His specialty was grilling, not frying vegetables and creating elaborate baked dishes. His pasta came prepared from the gourmet market these days.

As Marisa retrieved a spatula, he spied an ancient-looking KitchenAid mixer on her countertop, right next to the fixings for cupcakes.

"Your mixer looks like it's seen better days."

"You mean Kathy?"

"You named your mixer." He was careful to keep his tone neutral.

She adjusted a baking pan on the range with an oven mitt and then glanced at him over her shoulder. "It belonged to my grandmother. It's an heirloom, so it gets a name. In fact, *Nonna* let me name it when I was six. Kathy KitchenAid."

He watched her cut a piece of the eggplant parmigiana for him. Then he hooked his jacket over the back of a chair and took a seat at the well-worn kitchen table. Moments later Marisa set a steaming plate before him and handed him a fork.

The mozzarella was still oozing, and the breaded eggplant peeked out in thin layers—like a delicate *mille fiori* pastry.

He swallowed.

"Would you like a drink?" she asked.

He doubted she had beer on hand. "Water would be fine, thanks."

As Marisa walked to the fridge, he dug in with his fork and took his first bite. Her eggplant parmigiana went down smooth, hot and savory. *Fantastic.*

Apparently, Marisa could cook in the same way that Wayne Gretzky could play hockey.

Cole was four bites in and well on his way to demolishing her baked confection when she returned with a glass of water.

"Not sparkling water," she said apologetically, setting down a tumbler, "but filtered from the tap."

He filched a napkin from the stack on the table, wiped his mouth and then took a swallow.

He was here to seduce her, but she was enthralling him with her culinary skills. Her dish was sublime, and he'd do anything for a repeat of that kiss in the bar. "Marisa, you make an eggplant parmigiana that can reduce grown men to a drool and whimper."

She lowered her shoulders, and her mouth curved. "Don't the Serenghettis have a family recipe?"

"This may be even better, but don't tell my mother."

"I'm sure it's been decades since your mother tried to bring men to their knees. But I'm also certain she wouldn't mind if it was her eggplant parmigiana that did the trick."

"Yeah, she takes pride in her cooking." The truth was that while Camilla Serenghetti used food to lure her sons home, she was a force to be reckoned with in other ways, as well.

Marisa touched her hair. "I'll let you finish your food. I'll, um, be back in a few minutes."

"Sure." Moments later he heard a door click.

Cole finished the food before him, savoring every bite. When he was done, he got up and deposited his plate and glass in the sink—because if there was one thing Camilla Serenghetti had drilled into her sons, it was how to be polite and pick up after yourself.

Then he looked around and surveyed Marisa's place. It was unsporting of him, but he was willing to use any advantage to get to know more of her. Besides, he was curious about how she lived.

Walking out of the kitchen, he retraced his steps in the hallway. Marisa's bedroom door was closed. Beyond it, he entered the large living room. One corner held a desk, a bookcase and a screen that could be used to shield the nook from the rest of the room. A rolled-arm sofa upholstered in a cream-and-light-green stripe served as a counterpoint to the dominant flower motif. There were also several small tables that looked as if they could be hand-me-down family pieces—sturdy but with decades under their scarred chestnut tops.

From a builder's perspective, Marisa had done a good job sprucing up her prewar apartment without undertaking a major renovation. It was neat, cozy and feminine.

He walked over to a built-in bookshelf dotted with framed photos and found himself staring at a picture of Marisa the way she had looked in her high school days. She was laughing as she leaned against the railing of a pier. Wearing jeans and a sweatshirt, she appeared more relaxed and carefree than she'd been while roaming the halls at Pershing. With a sudden clenching of the gut, Cole wondered whether the photo had been snapped before or after the debacle of their senior year...

He glanced down at the books lining a shelf below eye level. Crouching, he tilted his head to read the titles. *Pleasing Your Man, Losing the Last 5 Lbs., The Infidelity Recovery Plan,* and last but not least, *Bad Boys and the Women Who Shouldn't Need Them.*

It didn't take a genius to make sense of the titles, especially since the final one seemed to be addressed to him personally.

Cole straightened. He'd never have guessed everything going on behind the facade of the normally reserved and occasionally fiery Marisa Danieli. He also couldn't believe his high school Lolita—edible as a sugared doughnut—saw herself as insufficiently sexy. Had ordering the Cobb salad at their dinner been about being thinner and more attractive? What about her exercise routine?

And what kind of jerk had she been engaged to? For sure, she'd had her ego bruised by Sal Piazza's horn-dog behavior. But if she thought Sal had strayed because she wasn't sexy enough, she was marching her feathered mules down the wrong school corridor. If Marisa could glimpse *his* fantasies lately, Cole was sure she'd overheat rather than doubt her sex appeal. He could happily lose his mind exploring her lush curves.

Hearing a sound behind him, he straightened and turned in time to see Marisa walk into the room, hair down and brushing her shoulders. "You've got an interesting collection of books."

Marisa's gaze moved from him to the bookcase, and she looked embarrassed.

"Sal wants to imitate the athletes that he represents," he said without preamble. "Sure he'd like to get his clients what they wish for, but he also wants to be them. That's why he wanted to bag Vicki. It wasn't about you."

"So don't take it personally?" she quipped.

"Those who can, do, and those who can't become sports agents instead," he responded without answering her directly.

"Like that saying about those who can, do, and those who can't, teach?" she parried. "Teaching is one of the hardest—"

"—jobs in the world," he finished for her. "I know. I was one of those problem students who got himself suspended, remember?"

After a moment, she sighed. "Those who can't become sports agents, and those who can't become teachers. So I guess Sal and I were perfectly matched."

He sauntered toward her, shaking his head. "I'm going to have to detox you."

"Oh no, you don't." She sidestepped him. "You come in and eat my food and read my books, and I still don't know why you're here."

"Don't you?"

"No, I don't!"

"You're a great cook," he said, trying a more subtle maneuver. "I got a sample today, and a couple of your students at the rink last week mentioned it. The kids also said you've brought your homemade dishes to school functions in the past."

She looked surprised and then embarrassed. "And now you have a burning desire for eggplant parmigiana?"

He let the word *desire* hang there between them.

"Everything I know I learned from my mother," she added after a moment.

"Great. My mother has a cooking show on a local cable channel. She's always looking for guests."

Marisa held up her hands. "I don't like where this is heading."

He flashed his teeth. "Oh yes, you do." He was becoming a pro at the tit-for-tat game that they had going on between them. "If I'm going to do the rooster strut at Pershing's big party, then you can cluck your way through a televised cooking show. Fair is fair."

"We already struck our bargain," she countered. "You want to renegotiate now? You're already getting the construction job for the gym, no questions asked."

"I'm prepared to offer something in return for your appearance under bright studio lights," he said nobly.

"And that would be?"

"I'll expand my offer from informal coaching to running that hockey clinic that you want."

She looked astonished. As if he could never tempt her to appear on TV—but he had.

He was willing to coach the kids without receiving anything in return, but he wasn't going to tell her that. He'd created another opportunity to interact with Marisa, and she was going to find it hard to say no. He was brilliant.

"It's a big investment of time. I'd need a good recipe, and then I'd have to prep for the show. The hair and makeup alone will take two or three hours…"

His lips inched upward. "You're starting to sound like I did about the hockey clinic."

"My mother is the real cook in the family," she protested.

"Great. We'll get her involved, too. It'll take the pressure off you."

"No!" She shook her head. "How did we get here? I haven't even agreed to be a part of this crazy plan."

"We'll do a giveaway." He warmed to his subject. "A set of Stanhope Department Store's own stainless-steel cookware that retails for hundreds of dollars. You said your mother was the new housewares buyer, right? It'll be great promo. Move over, Oprah."

He was beyond brilliant.

"I'm busy right now. Parent-teacher conferences. The fund-raiser. The end of the school year… And I'm painting my kitchen cabinets before the weather gets hot because I don't have central air in this condo."

He glanced around them. "Yeah, you've got a retro vibe going."

"I like to call it modern vintage."

He wasn't familiar with the style but he was appreciating Marisa's '50s-style apron, and he had another great idea. "I'll help with the painting."

"You don't need to help. We're not dating."

He shrugged. "This isn't dating. This is an exchange of favors."

"Is that what you called your involvement with Vicki?" she parried. "An exchange of favors?"

He gave a semblance of a smile. "Oh, sweet pea, you're asking for it. Detox, it is."

"And you're going to provide the cure?" she scoffed. "It's pretty clear you're a womanizer."

"I enjoy women, yes. Therapy may be needed later, but right now I'm hung up on teachers with attitude."

"I know a great therapist," she said, her voice all sugar.

"And I've got a better idea for how to deal with our hang-ups."

She parted her lips, but before she could answer him, he pulled her into his arms and captured her mouth.

Marisa stilled, and then she kissed Cole back. She slid her arms around his neck, and her fingers threaded into his hair. He tasted of her baking, but underneath was the unmistakable scent of pure male.

One second she'd been fighting her attraction to him, and the next she'd been overwhelmed by it.

He held her firmly as his tongue stroked around hers. She pressed into him, her breasts yielding, and she felt the hard bulge of his arousal. Her mind clouded, waves of sensation washing over her.

Cole ended the kiss, and she moaned. But he trailed his lips down the side of her throat and then moved back up to suck on her earlobe. His breath next to her ear sent shivers chasing through her. Her breasts, and the most sensitive spot between her legs, felt heavy with need.

She tugged Cole back for another searing kiss. She felt the arm of the sofa behind her and realized that with one small tip, they could fall onto it.

He lifted his mouth from hers. "Tell me to leave now. Otherwise, this is going to end up where I want."

"And where would that be?"

He looked down at her clothes. "I'll be the guy who satisfies your inner domestic goddess."

Wow. His words served to arouse her further.

He gave a slow-burn smile and nodded at her ruffly apron. "I couldn't have dreamed of a sexier get-up if I tried."

"It's meant for cooking," she protested.

"Among other things." His hands settled on her waist, and he rocked against her as he bent and nuzzled her neck. "You didn't tell me to leave."

She couldn't. She tried to force the words, but they wouldn't come.

"You're beautiful and sexy and alluring. I want to be inside you, pleasing us both until you're calling out my name again and again…"

Oh. My. Sweet. Heaven. His words set her on fire. With Sal, sex had always been perfunctory. He'd never given her words…

Cole cupped her buttocks and lifted her, pressing her against him.

She cradled his face and kissed him again.

"Bed," he said thickly, "though the sofa would work, too."

"Mmm," she mumbled.

He must have taken her response for a yes because the next thing she knew, she perched on the back edge of the sofa.

Cole covered one of her breasts with his hand. He shaped and molded the sensitized mound and its taut peak. Then he trailed moist kisses down her throat and along her collarbone.

Releasing her breast, he tugged at the hem of her tee. She helped him, and then they both worked to slide the top over her head.

Cole's gaze settled on her chest, and she tried not to squirm. She'd always been self-conscious about her size.

"You're even more beautiful than I remembered," he breathed.

Then he bent his head and drew one tight bud into his mouth, bra and all, sucking her as if enraptured.

Oh. Oh. Oh. She didn't think she was going to last. She needed Cole now. She ached for him, already halfway to release even though he'd only put his mouth on her.

When he lifted his head, he blew against her breast, and if possible, her nipple grew tighter against its thin and wet covering. Marisa nearly came out of her skin.

Cole unclasped her bra and pulled it off her. He ducked his head and took her breast deep into his mouth, laving her with his tongue and then swirling it around her nipple.

Marisa pulled his head close. Sal had never given her body this level of attentiveness while Cole acted as if he had all the time in the world. Fifteen years ago she'd held Cole to her breast like this. But now he was all man—strong, capable and sure of himself. The scar across his cheek was pulled taught, and the stubble on his face was a gentle abrasion against her skin.

She gripped his head as he transferred his attention to her other breast. Her head fell back, and her eyes fluttered closed. With the world shut out, only Cole and his touch existed, with an even greater intensity than before.

Cole lifted his head, and his breath hissed out. "What do you want, Marisa?"

She opened her eyes to meet his. "You know."

"I want to hear you say it."

"You. I want you."

A look of satisfaction crossed his face. "Some things don't change, sweet pea. I can't keep my hands off you, either."

In response, she guided his hands back to her breasts, where they could both feel her racing heart.

"Marisa, Marisa," he muttered.

He was all appreciation, and it was like a salve to her soul. She'd never felt like a goddess before, domestic or otherwise.

He gave her a gentle nudge, and she slid off the back edge of the sofa and onto the seat cushions, her legs dangling off one arm. Her mules hit the carpet with one muffled thud after another.

Cole pushed up her apron and then pulled off her biker shorts with one fluid movement. He stroked up her thigh, his calluses a shivery roughness against her skin—reminding her that he had a physical job as well as an office one.

"Ah, Marisa." Pushing aside her underwear, he pressed his thumb against her most sensitive spot while his finger probed and then slipped inside her.

She gasped. "What are you doing?"

"What does it seem like I'm doing?" he murmured, his thumb sweeping and pressing in a rhythm that made her tighten unbearably. "I'm going to make you breathless, sweet pea."

"Make me?"

It was the last thing she said before she gave herself up to sensation. Within moments she convulsed around him, her hips bucking. It was an orgasm born of a forbidden longing that had been brewing for fifteen years.

When she subsided, she realized Cole had satisfied her, but not himself. Her gaze connected with his, and she took in the intense expression stamped there.

"Yes," he said huskily. "It's going to be even better than before."

Better than before.

Marisa heard a knock at the front door, but in her sexual haze, it took her a moment to react. Then she froze.

Cole stilled, as well, apparently having heard the same thing.

There was the distinct sound of a key being slipped into the front door and the lock turning.

Marisa's eyes widened and fixed on Cole's.

In the next instant she was scrambling off the sofa—swinging her legs down and around and bolting to her feet.

Cole tossed her the biker shorts, but she had no time to do anything but stuff them under a pillow as she brushed down her apron.

"Marisa?" Serafina called. "Hello?"

Her cousin appeared in the entrance to the living room, and Marisa thought the whole situation could take the prize for *Most Awkward Situation in One's Own Home*.

Serafina blinked. "Oh...hello."

Marisa prayed her face didn't betray her. "Um, hi, Sera. I didn't know you were going to stop by."

"I overlooked a couple of small things when I moved out." Sera shrugged. "Since I still had the emergency key to the apartment, I thought it would be no problem if I showed up on my way to work. I did knock."

It was as if they were both pretending there wasn't a six-foot-plus sexy guy standing in the corner of her living room.

Marisa glanced at Cole, who was shielded by the high back of an armchair. She had no such cover. She hoped her apron was enough to disguise the fact that she was wearing only underwear. "Sera, you know Cole Serenghetti, don't you?"

Her cousin's gaze moved to Cole. "I thought I recognized you."

"Nice to meet one of Marisa's relatives."

Sera nodded. "I'm going to...go search the kitchen for my small blender."

"Sure, go right ahead," Marisa chirped. "I thought I saw it in there."

When her cousin turned and left, Marisa breathed a sigh of relief. Cole tossed the biker shorts at her, and she slipped into them while avoiding his eyes.

"I'll let myself out," he announced wryly.

"We shouldn't have done this," she blurted. *Nothing had changed.* She was as easy a conquest for him as she'd always been. Willing to stop, drop and roll anytime, anywhere.

Cole ran a hand through his hair. "Get rid of the books on the shelf. You don't need them."

Marisa stared at him. It was a typical understated and sardonic Cole Serenghetti compliment. She wasn't sure whether to hug it close, or run for cover.

"I'll let you know the timing for the television show." Giving her one last significant look, Cole strode from the room.

Moments later Marisa heard her front door open and close for the second time. Taking a deep breath, she walked toward the back of the apartment. She found Serafina in the kitchen, opening and closing cabinets.

"I know that little handheld blender and juicer is in here somewhere…"

"Have you tried the cabinet above the stove?"

Serafina turned and gave her a once-over. "Well, you look fit for company again. At least the nonmale version."

"Cole came over because we had things to…discuss about the fund-raiser. And because he's looking for a couple of guests for his mother's cooking show, and I'm trying to get him to run a hockey clinic for the kids." *And I kissed him at the Puck & Shoot, and I hope the news doesn't spread…or hasn't already to you.* Fortunately, since she'd never been to the Puck & Shoot before last week, there was no reason for anyone to recognize her as Sera's cousin and make a connection.

Her cousin tilted her head. "And those, uh, discussions happened with your pants off?"

Marisa flushed. *Busted.*

Serafina lifted her eyebrows. "He's hot, for sure. And at least he doesn't have his brother's reputation for going through women as if he needs to spread the love."

"I—"

"You need a bodyguard. You obviously can't be trusted, or he can't—or the both of you. I'm not sure which it is. It looks like he's forgiven you for high school and then some."

"It's not what you think." *It was pretend—or some of it was.* Sera seemingly hadn't gotten the bulletin yet that Marisa had kissed Cole at the Puck & Shoot, or her cousin would have mentioned it already.

"Wow, and we've descended into cliché, too. Give me a sec—I need to wrap my mind around this one. Maybe a bodyguard and a therapist? I can hunt up recommendations for you."

Marisa sighed. "C'mon, Sera."

"Well, you two have definitely got a thing for one another."

"We don't, really." The denial sounded weak, even to her own ears. *Ugh.*

"He wants you to appear on his mother's cooking show? That's serious."

"It's not as if I'm showing up as a member of the family."

"Just be careful. You two have a complicated past."

"I know."

"Great. Then that's settled." Sera gave an exaggerated sigh of relief. "Phew!"

"There's one tiny wrinkle."

Her cousin stilled. "Oh?"

"We're pretending to be a couple."

Sera's eyes widened. "That's not a wrinkle. That's a—"

"Really. We're faking it."

Sera jerked her thumb in the direction of the living room. "So you two were pretending to go at it in there?"

"No, yes… I mean, our relationship is fake!"

She filled in her cousin on what had happened at the Puck & Shoot, ending with her pact with Cole not to correct the perception that they were an item, at least until the Pershing Shines Bright benefit. Even as she told her story to Sera, Marisa admitted to herself that she had to try harder not to blur the line between reality and make-believe.

When she finished, Sera regarded her for an instant, head tilted to the side. "I wouldn't want to see you get hurt again."

"I'm not in high school anymore."

"No, but you still work there, and Cole has had another fifteen years to hone his lady-killer skills. Plus, he's admitted he wished things had turned out differently between you at Pershing."

"I told him I couldn't get involved. He knows the Danieli family history with professional athletes."

"If that's the reason you're hiding behind, go better. Cole is retired from pro hockey."

"Yes, but running the family construction business is a temporary sideline for him." She didn't want anything to do with someone who still had his hand in pro sports. She's made a good life for herself, right here in Welsdale.

"Well, you could become a temporary sideline to the temporary sideline. There's your reason to be wary."

Marisa threw up her hands. "You and Jordan should try Scrabble. Word play is your thing."

"What?"

"Never mind."

Eight

Marisa had done hard things in her life. Growing up, she'd sometimes been two short steps from foraging in a trash bin for food. But meeting Cole's family on the set of his mother's show, amid swirling rumors of their new status as a couple, trumped stealing away with a supermarket's barely expired eggs, in her opinion.

She hoped Cole had a good story to tell everybody about how they'd started dating.

"Relax," Cole said, giving her a quick peck on the cheek as she stepped onto the set. "It's fine."

"Then why is Jordan giving me a knowing look?" she responded sotto voce, nodding to where Jordan occupied an empty seat where the audience normally sat.

Cole caught his brother's bemused expression. "This situation is rife for humor, and he knows it." He frowned at Jordan, who gave a jaunty little wave in response.

"Don't worry, I'll pound the jokes out of him in the ring next week."

Marisa turned away. "I'm going home. I can't do this."

Cole took hold of her arm. "Oh yes, you can."

"Cole, introduce me, please!"

Marisa swung back in time to see Camilla Serenghetti approaching them.

Too late.

Anyone could have guessed this was Cole's mother. Mother and son shared similar coloring and had the same eyes. Marisa had never had an opportunity to meet Cole's parents while she'd been at Pershing, but she'd glimpsed them in the stands at hockey games.

"Either she's the forgive-and-forget kind," she murmured to Cole, "or she's so thankful to see you in a relationship, she's willing to overlook anything."

Cole grinned. "Draw your own conclusions, sweet pea."

"Let's see, Italian mother, no grandkids…" Marisa was too familiar with the dynamics from her own family. "I choose the latter."

"She doesn't know about your part in my suspension," Cole replied in a low voice. "I did a good job of keeping her in the dark about my inner life as a teenager."

Marisa cast him a sidelong look. "So she doesn't know we—"

"—tested out the therapeutic properties of the theater department's couch?"

Cole arched a brow, and she flushed.

Cole shook his head. "No."

"Still," Marisa whispered back, "I know, and it's enough."

Cole's poor mother. First, Marisa had gotten her son suspended. And now she'd drafted him to star in a faux relationship. She could barely keep herself from cringing.

"Watch this," Cole said.

Marisa looked at him questioningly as he bestowed a broad smile on his mother.

"Mom, meet Marisa. She makes an eggplant parmigiana that rivals yours."

Marisa took a deep breath. *Well.* "I learned everything from my mother."

Camilla clapped. "Wonderful. I'm so glad she's comin' on my program, too."

"She should be here any minute. And my mother has seen your show, Mrs. Serenghetti. In fact, both she and I have watched numerous episodes."

She was a glutton for punishment. She avoided Cole's eyes, but heat stained her cheeks. She was a pushover for cooking shows. The fact that the host of this one was Cole Serenghetti's mother was beside the point. At least that was her story, and she was sticking to it. She purposely hadn't sought out news of Cole over the years, but when she'd stumbled upon an episode of *Flavors of Italy* more than a year ago, she'd been hooked.

"Please, call me Camilla. I've been trying to get Cole and Jordan to come back on the show for a long time."

Marisa looked inquiringly at Cole. "You don't want to be on your mother's show again?"

He'd been on the program at least once—how had she missed that episode? It must have been one of the early ones. She should be glad she missed it, so why did she feel disappointed?

Cole raised an eyebrow. "I can only work on saving one parent at a time."

Oh right—the construction company. Marisa could relate—how often had she worried about her mother? Family ties could bind, but they also had the potential to choke.

"You live in Welsdale, Marisa?" Camilla asked.

"Yes, I have my own condo on Chestnut Street."

Camilla looked perplexed. "You live alone?"

"My cousin Serafina was my roommate until recently."

Cole's mother appeared slightly mollified. "Well, is something."

"My mother thinks living alone is wrong," Cole said drolly. "We had lots of relatives on extended stays with us when I was growing up. You could say my mother never got out of the hotel business, even after marriage."

"Cole, don't be fresh."

"What? I'm wrong?"

"Your cousin Allegra is coming to visit with her family this fall."

"And I rest my case," Cole said.

Camilla adopted a slightly wounded look. "My children moved out. There's room."

Marisa was saved from saying anything, however, by the arrival of her own mother.

The family party was just getting started... Jordan Serenghetti, for one, had graduated from looking entertained to outright amused.

Donna Casale glanced around the set and then walked to where Marisa was standing with Cole and

Camilla Serenghetti. Scanning the empty audience chairs, she said, "I must be early. There's hardly anyone here. Oh well, at least we can nab the best seats!"

Marisa stepped forward. "Actually, Mom, there isn't going to be an audience." Unless you counted Jordan's avid spectating. "This isn't a taping."

Donna looked confused.

"We're not going to be part of the audience, we're going to be guests on the show." She added weakly, "Surprise!"

Jordan guffawed.

Marisa fixed a smile on her face, willing her mother to go along. She hadn't said anything about their guest appearance because she'd wanted to avoid too many questions. Plus, she figured the element of surprise would work to her advantage because her mother wouldn't have a chance to get intimidated and say no.

Donna's eyes widened. "We're going to be on TV?"

Marisa grabbed her hand. "Yes! Isn't it great?" She needed all the enthusiasm she could muster in order to keep nerves at bay. "Let me introduce you to Camilla Serenghetti…and her sons."

Introductions were made, and Marisa was relieved that everyone seemed to relax a little. Her mother actually started to appear happy at the prospect of making an appearance on a program that she watched.

Marisa cleared her throat. "And Cole has this great idea that we can do a giveaway on air as an advertisement for Stanhope Department Stores. What do you think, Mom?"

Her mother looked at her speculatively and then smiled. "I'll bring it up with management at work, but I'm sure they'll be thrilled."

Marisa lowered her shoulders, but Cole seemed bemused.

"You didn't tell your mother that she was about to become a star?" he murmured.

"Stop it," she responded in a low voice.

"Mmm, interesting. The first time you've asked me to stop." The sexual suggestion in his voice was unmistakable. "The words never crossed your lips in the storage room, or at the bar…or in your apartment, come to think of it."

"St—" She caught herself and compressed her mouth. "You're enjoying this."

"There are a lot of things I enjoy…doing with you."

Marisa felt a wave of awareness swamp her. Fortunately, their mothers appeared to be deep in their own conversation, because she could barely look at Cole. She grew hot at the memory of what they had done on her couch, which she'd now taken to referring to as Couch #2—never to be confused with the chintzy Couch #1 that still resided at the Pershing School. Whenever the student theater group had used #1 in a play over the years, Marisa could hardly keep her mind on the performance.

And right now Cole looked primed and ready for another round. Except she wasn't about to defile his mother's TV set sofa, no matter how hungry and frustrated Cole was.

She suppressed a giggle that welled up from nowhere and forced her mind back to the topic at hand. Camilla and her mother were engaged in a brisk discussion about whether to make a *tiella* or a *calzone di cipolla* on the air. The potato-and-mussel casserole and the onion pie were both dishes of Puglia, the Italian region of Marisa's ancestors.

"The calzone is a traditional Christmas recipe," Donna said. "Like plum pudding in England. And since this show is going to air in the spring, I think the *tiella* would be better."

Marisa had told her mother to bring a couple of recipes along today, and had discussed them with her in advance. Her little white lie had been that the show planned to enter audience members in a raffle giveaway if they brought along a recipe.

"Donna, *cara, siamo d'accordo!*"

Cole's mother's enthusiasm and agreement were apparent no matter what the language spoken. Still... *Donna, cara*? When had her mother and Cole's progressed to being bosom buddies?

"You will be *perfetto* on the show, Donna. You and the *bellissima* Marisa."

Marisa felt Cole lean close.

"I'm surprised she isn't suggesting you become a bottle blonde," he murmured sardonically, "like the rest of the hostesses on Italian television."

"This is not an Italian show, Cole!" His mother fixed him with a look that said she'd overheard. "My hair is brown, and I speak English."

"Some people would debate the second part."

"Uh-oh," Jordan singsonged from his seat in the front row. "Cole's gonna be barred from the lasagna dinners."

"Exactly what is your role here?" Cole shot back.

Jordan grinned. "Comic relief. And Mom invited me." He looked around. "Hey, where's the popcorn? The drama's been good up to now, but the concessions leave something to be desired."

Cole ignored his brother and turned toward Marisa and her mother. "What my mother means is that she thinks Mrs. Casale has the personality for television. It's important to engage the audience on the small screen."

"Yes," Camilla agreed. "And dress in bold *colori* but not too much zigzag or *fiori*."

"Chill on the patterns," Jordan piped up.

"Makeup—more is better."

"I'm so glad we're doing this," Donna remarked with enthusiasm. "Marisa has loved to cook and bake since she was a little girl."

"Cole loved to eat," Camilla confided.

"Marisa was born a preemie, so I spent the first few months making sure she put on weight!"

Marisa bit her lip. "Oh, Mom, not that story again." Her mother had a terrifying habit of bringing it up in public situations.

"Scrappy, that's what I've always called her."

"Cole was nine pounds. Was a long labor," Camilla put in.

"Why doesn't anyone think of sharing those types of details on a date?" Cole quipped to Marisa.

"Maybe because you're too busy admiring your date's inner domestic goddess?" she shot back in a low voice before she could stop herself.

Cole gave her a half-lidded look. "Yeah…there's that distraction."

"Your mother is hilarious," she sidestepped.

"Larger than life. It makes her perfect for television."

As if on cue, his mother interjected, "Marisa, *bella*, you will come to the party in two weeks, *si*?"

What? What party?

"Ah…yes." She gave the only answer she could with three pairs of Serenghetti eyes on her.

"I ask your mother already, but she's going to a wedding tha' day."

"Ted's cousin's daughter is getting married," Donna explained in response to Marisa's inquiring look.

"Right." How could she forget? And now it seemed as if she was going to be flying solo with the Serenghettis.

"*Grazie per l'invito*, Camilla," Donna said. "Another time."

"Your mother speaks Italian?" Cole asked.

"She grew up in an Italian-speaking household," Marisa responded distractedly because she was still dwelling on the invite to the Serenghettis' domain.

Camilla perked up. "Cole knows Italian. We did *vacanze in Italia* when he was young."

Marisa figured that explained why Cole hadn't been in her Italian classes at Pershing.

"You speak *italiano*, Marisa?"

"*Abbastanza.*"

Camilla clasped her hands together, and shot a glance at her eldest son. "Enough. Wonderful."

Marisa could swear her expression said *she's perfetto*, but Cole just looked droll.

Fortunately for her, the show's producers interrupted at that point, and the conversation veered in another direction. But once the details of their guest appearance had been hammered out—and the appropriate forms and releases signed for the show's producers—Marisa moved toward the exit.

Unfortunately, Cole stood between her and the door.

"What are you doing this weekend?" he asked without preamble.

"Why do you ask?" she hedged, even though they weren't within earshot of Jordan or their mothers, who remained engrossed in conversation on the studio's stage.

"This weekend I'm having the first meeting of that hockey clinic that we talked about," he said. "But I prefer the rest of my time not be spent with a bunch of teenagers."

"You'd never make it as a teacher."

"I think we've established that," he responded drily. "But I pegged you for one who'd be teaching economics."

"After high school, I knew I'd never really understand economics."

"You seemed to be doing okay to me."

"Right. As if you were in a good position to judge."

He smiled. "We were both distracted back then, but I'm not going to apologize for being a major diversion for you. Speaking of which, how about dinner at Agosto at seven this Saturday?"

"I'm painting my kitchen cabinets."

"You're kidding."

She shook her head.

"I've been turned down for dates before—"

She feigned astonishment.

"—but never because someone needed to paint the kitchen cabinets."

"This relationship has been a land of firsts." She could have bitten her tongue. Of all the firsts, him being her *first* lover was at the top of the list. And from his expression, the thought had hit him, too.

"You, me, a can of paint. I can't think of a kinkier combination."

She rolled her eyes even as she tingled at his words. He'd switched gears smoothly from suggesting dinner at a fine restaurant…to making painting seem adventurous.

"I hope you chose a red-hot shade. Make Me Magenta. Or Kiss & Cuddle Coral."

"You know, I'd never thought of the building business as sexy, but now I see how wrong I've been. Just buying paint must leave you breathless!"

A slow smile spread across his face. "If you invite me over, you can find out what else leaves me breathless."

"I was planning on painting the cabinets by myself."

He looked her over. "Why bother when you have a sexy construction guy to do it with?"

She was starting to feel hot again—and very, very breathless. Damn him. He knew what he was doing, but he was also keeping a straight face. "I don't have the money to hire someone. That's why I was planning to do it alone."

"For you, sweet pea, I come free."

"The kitchen cabinets are a little dreary," she said unnecessarily, trying to cool things down.

"Add color to your life."

She'd paint *him* red—he was definitely a red. "The cabinets are going to be yellow. Unblemished Sapphire Yellow."

He cut off a laugh. "I guess I shouldn't be surprised."

"I've already bought the paint supplies."

"Great. When do we start?"

"I start on Saturday morning." She hoped she sounded repressive enough.

"I'll be there at eight."

* * *

When Marisa opened the door to her apartment on Saturday morning, Cole was holding a container with coffee cups and assorted add-ins. He grasped a brown paper bag with his other hand.

"Doughnuts," he announced. "A construction industry morning tradition."

"Thank you," she said, taking the bag from him.

She stepped back so he could enter the apartment, and her heartbeat picked up. He was strong, solid and masculine. And yummy. *Forbidden, but yummy.* He looked great in paint-stained jeans, work boots and an open flannel shirt over a white tee.

By contrast, she'd dressed in a green tee and an old pair of gray sweats. She'd used a scrunchie to pull her hair back in a ponytail. With no makeup or jewelry, she hardly felt sexy—though she still itched with need at the sight of him.

"I'd show you to the kitchen, but we'll be working in there, not…eating." A sudden image flashed through her mind of Cole slipping his hands under her tee and up her midriff, moving ever closer to her breasts…

Wow, it was hot in here.

She led the way into the living room and then turned back toward him.

"Let me take the coffee from you," she said, intending to set the coffee carrier down on the wood tray that covered a rectangular ottoman.

Their fingers brushed, and her eyes flew up to meet his. They both stilled, and then he leaned in and touched her lips with his.

"You're welcome," he said in a low voice as he straightened.

"I thought we'd keep up the pretense about painting at least until nine." She set down the coffee and faced him again.

"Sex first thing in the morning is great," he responded, "and I've been saving it all for you."

"I thought sports guys abstained from sex before a big game in order to keep their edge." If he was going to expend a lot of effort today on painting, wasn't it a similar situation?

"Sweet pea, I don't play professionally anymore, and you'll never see a better painter after this," he responded with heartfelt enthusiasm.

She gave a nervous laugh—because he did make her tense. And aroused. And crazy. It was hard not to be thrilled with a guy who lusted after her even when she looked as if she was going to haul out the garbage. Even if her mind told her she shouldn't.

He stepped forward and cupped her face, his fingers threading into her hair and loosening her ponytail. Gazing at her mouth, he muttered, "You know, I used to steal glances at you when we were working on that presentation for economics class. Just for the sheer pleasure of looking at you."

"Really?" she breathed.

He nodded, and then gave her another light kiss.

When he straightened, she swallowed. "I could tell you were staring at me sometimes… I thought I had a food smudge or a blemish, or you were wondering why my face wasn't completely symmetrical—"

His eyes crinkled. "Marisa?"

"Yes?"

"Adolescent boys think about one thing, and it's not

about looking in the bathroom mirror for hours and searching for flaws."

"Oh, and what do you think about?" she asked, even though she had a good idea.

"This."

He claimed her lips for a deeper kiss. He traced the seam of her mouth and then slipped inside. She breathed in his warm, male scent and then met his tongue, leaning into him. The power of the kiss seeped into her.

She followed his lead, meeting him again and again, until she was in a pleasant languor, her head swimming. When they broke apart, she bent her head, her forehead coming to rest against his lips.

He settled his hands on her waist and then slipped them under the bottom of her sweatshirt. He kneaded her flesh, caressing her back and rubbing up to her shoulder blades. With a deft move, he unclasped her bra and she spilled against him.

Raising his mouth a fraction from her forehead, he muttered, "Marisa."

"What?" she asked dreamily.

"I've fantasized about your breasts."

"Now?"

"Now. High school. Forever."

"Mmm."

He pulled the sweatshirt over her head, and she took out the scrunchie holding her hair, shaking her head to loosen the strands.

Gazing down at her, he said, "You still have the prettiest breasts I've ever seen."

"And on a schoolteacher, no less. Go figure," she joked.

"Luscious Lola. You live up to your nickname."

"What?"

He raised his eyes. "You didn't know? It's what the guys in the locker room called you. But we couldn't agree on how big your breasts were because you had a habit of hugging books to your chest."

Her eyes widened. "You're kidding."

He gave her a teasing smile. "Nope. The nickname Luscious Lola was sort of tongue-in-cheek. The imaginations of teenage boys can outstrip reality." His look turned appreciative. "Not in this case, however."

"I didn't even know I existed in the jocks' locker room!"

"Oh, you existed, all right."

"You gave out nicknames?" She still couldn't believe it. She'd thought she'd been invisible in high school—well, at least until the end.

Cole shrugged.

"Well, you eventually found out how big my breasts were. But I couldn't figure out why you didn't broadcast the news…"

He sobered. "By that point, it was too heavy to share. I'd started thinking of you as my personal Lolita. The girl who slew me and led to my destruction."

"And now?" she asked, curious and a little wary, even as she adopted a tone of mock reproach. "Am I still just a sex object with big breasts?"

He looked into her eyes. "And now you're the woman I've been fantasizing about. *Ti voglio.* I want to make love to you, Marisa."

When he held out his hand, she went weak and then put her hand in his. If she was honest with herself, she'd admit this moment had been inevitable ever since Cole had announced he'd help her paint. The last time he'd been in her apartment, they'd ended up tangled together on her living room couch until Sera's unexpected arrival. She could have done more to avert this moment if she'd wanted to, but in the secret recesses of her heart, she knew she'd always wanted to deal with the unfinished business between her and Cole.

Cole threw some pillows on the floor and tugged her down to their makeshift bed, where they both kneeled and faced each other. He gently pulled her into his embrace, and then he kissed her, one arm anchored around her waist, the other caressing her breast.

Marisa moaned, her scruples evaporating. Cole's thumb toyed with her nipple, causing sensation to shoot through her and pool between her legs.

"Cole," she gasped, her fingers threading through his hair, "please."

"Please, what?" he asked gutturally.

"Now, more…"

"Yes."

She lay back against the pillows, and he pulled off his shirt and then tugged the white tee over his head.

Marisa sucked in a breath. He was *built*. Bigger and broader than in high school, but solid muscle nonetheless. He might have left the ice, but he seemed as toned and ready for action as ever. He had flat abs, and sculpted muscles outlined his upper arms. She'd gotten a partial look at Jimmy's Boxing Gym, but unclothed, he was even more spectacular.

He gazed at her with glittering promise. Then he grasped the waistband of her sweatpants and pulled them off, taking her panties, socks and canvas lace-ups with them.

Tossing her clothes aside, he moved back to her and

stroked a hand down her thigh. He raised her leg, flexed her foot and placed a kiss on the delicate skin behind her knee. "You've got a fantastic figure, sweet pea. Made for loving."

She'd dreamed about this moment in the past. She'd wondered what would have happened if things had turned out differently—if her relationship with Cole had survived to become a real adult one.

For his part, Cole looked like a man who'd reached an oasis and wasn't going to hold back. He stood and pulled off his shoes and then stripped off the rest of his clothes. When she held out her arms, he came down beside her.

He claimed her mouth again, and she ran her hands over his arms, feeling his muscles move and flex beneath her fingertips. His erection pressed against her, cradled between her thighs.

How many times after high school had she replayed their one time together? The truth was she'd never completely put him behind her.

When the kiss broke off, she touched his cheek. "You explained the knee injury that stopped your career with the Razors. But you never said how you got the scar."

Cole's look turned sardonic. "Simple. Another player's blade connected with my mug."

She frowned and then traced the long, white line bisecting the side of his face. "Have you ever thought of getting it fixed?"

"Nah...and have my good looks marred by cosmetic surgery?"

Impulsively leaning up, she trailed featherlight kisses along his scar. When she was finished, Cole looked as if he'd been undone.

"Ah, Marisa," he said gruffly. "That was…sweet."

"Women would die to have your nonchalant attitude about their physical appearance." She paused. "Women would die to have you, come to think of it."

He gave her a lopsided grin. "After our first time in high school, I used to think about ways to make the experience better the next time."

"You did?"

He nodded. "Yup. I still have a game plan filed away that I never got to use."

She sighed dreamily.

He stroked her arms. "Close your eyes, Marisa. Just feel."

When her eyes had fluttered closed, Cole began to massage her back, loosening her muscles and making her relax. Slowly, she came away from the edge of nervous arousal to something deeper and more soul-stirring.

Cole kissed her and then trailed his mouth down the column of her neck. He paused, blew on her nipples and then laved one with his tongue. When she jerked, he shushed her, gentling her with his hands. Then he drew her other breast into his mouth.

Awash in pleasure, Marisa threaded her hands in his hair, holding him. She felt fantasy merge with reality. Cole was here, making love to her. How many times had she dreamed about it? It was like her fantasies, but better in many ways… He was sure of himself, confident in his ability to please her. The full adult version of the teenager she had known.

"We'll never use a real bed," she murmured.

Cole stifled a laugh. "All in good time, including the kitchen, eventually."

She opened her eyes. "I cook in the kitchen."

"Me, too."

"Not that type of cooking."

"Ah, Marisa." He moved downward and kissed one inner thigh and then the other. Then he pressed his lips against her moist core. He found her with his mouth and caressed and swirled her with his tongue.

She moaned, and her hips rose, but Cole held her to him, his hands under her rear end.

She turned her head to muffle her moans against a pillow as sensation swamped her. But it was too much. Panting, she gave in, and let the world explode as she bucked against Cole's mouth.

Seconds later, spent, she collapsed back against their makeshift bed.

Cole came back up to face her. "It's not over until you're completely sexually satisfied."

Oh. "I need a moment." Her heart was racing, and she could still feel his arousal against her. "You have incredible staying power."

"In hockey and in business, it's about self-control. Like life, generally." He smiled, smoothing her hair. "But don't sell yourself short. You have wonderful stamina yourself."

"You've always had a lot of self-control around me." She knew she sounded wistful, but he'd been able to turn away from her so easily fifteen years ago…

"No, I don't," he corrected on a growl. "Let me show you."

Standing up, Cole withdrew a foil packet from the pocket of his jeans and sheathed himself. Tossing her a rueful grin, he said, "Wishful thinking, but I came prepared."

Marisa licked dry lips. With Sal, it had always been plain-vanilla sex—on a bed, at night and over quickly. She was unprepared for Cole's lustiness, though she'd be lying to herself if she said she didn't like it.

In the next moment Cole flipped her on her stomach and grasped her legs, spreading them as he pulled her to the edge of the pillows. He leaned forward, bracing himself over her, and his erection probed her entrance.

"You are so hot and slick," he breathed beside her ear. "So ready for me."

She felt him slide into her without any resistance and cried out at his possession, while Cole gave a labored groan behind her. He thrust into her once, twice, three times, and she called his name.

He set up a rhythm for them, pumping into her. "Marisa."

She could feel him tightening, and could tell he was close to finding his climax. She clamped down around him, and he cursed. Then they were both spiraling, the air filled with the sounds of their release.

She cried out as she crested on a wave of sensation so pure and beautiful—its power building for fifteen years—that tears stung her eyes.

After a moment, Cole slumped on top of her. Then he kissed her ear and rolled to his side, bringing her with him into the shelter of his body.

Marisa waited for her heart to slow down. Cole had given her one of the most spectacular experiences of her life. She was caught between joy at the wonder of it and embarrassment at her uninhibited response.

"Was that the game plan that you had filed away for fifteen years?" she asked.

He gave a helpless laugh. "Part of it."

There was more? Still, she managed, "It was so much better than on a regular bed."

He smiled against her hair. "I told you it would be better with a sexy construction guy."

Nine

If Marisa had any doubt that she and Cole had grown up in very different circumstances, they were erased when she entered his parents' house—a Mediterranean villa set amidst beautiful landscaping with a stone fountain at the center of a circular drive. She could almost believe she was in Tuscany, which she'd backpacked through one summer.

Still, she'd been nervous about this party ever since Camilla had issued her invite. She'd debated what to wear and had settled on a shirt and short skirt. Cole had driven to her apartment building, and she'd met him downstairs in the entry, not trusting the two of them in her condo alone even for a few minutes. Seeing him in a shirt and khakis, she'd been reassured that she'd at least dressed appropriately.

Thanks to Cole, her kitchen had gotten a wonderful

facelift. After their romantic interlude, they had gotten on with the job of painting, and she'd discovered Cole knew much more about the intricacies of stripping old paint and dealing with molding than she did. Her kitchen looked great—and he'd worked magic on her, too.

Marisa followed Cole through gleaming rooms decorated with a bow to the Serenghettis' Italian heritage to the back of the villa. When they reached his parents' backyard, she took in the impressive outdoor kitchen, blue-stone patio under a striped awning and wrought-iron furniture. It was an unseasonably warm day in May, and the Serenghetti party was mostly an outdoor affair. People milled about, glasses in hand, and platters of food had been set out on most flat surfaces.

Marisa looked over at her construction guy. Though when she'd started thinking of Cole as hers, she couldn't quite say. It was a telling slip that was *dangerous*. They'd had spectacular sex that had transported her from her comfort zone to an area where she was vulnerable, exposed and swamped with emotion and sensation. But still, she couldn't—shouldn't—attach too much importance to it. She had once in high school, and she'd fallen flat on her face. She also hoped it wasn't obvious to everyone that they'd recently become lovers for the first—no, second—time.

Cole placed his hand at the small of her back, and Marisa glanced at him. He wasn't trying to be subtle about their connection—though which of the two of them was a fraud was hard to tell. Weren't they supposed to pretend to be a couple? It was getting so confusing...

Cole bent for a quick kiss. "I'm glad you're here."

"There are more of you Serenghettis than I've ever seen in one place," Marisa responded, wondering how many people had seen that peck on the lips.

Cole laughed. "Don't worry, they don't bite—" he bent to murmur in her ear "—unlike me."

On her quick intake of breath, he straightened, his eyes gleaming.

Quelling the sudden hot-and-bothered feeling, Marisa scanned the crowd. She had known in high school that Cole had three younger siblings, but she hadn't been friends with any of them. She'd heard a bit about Jordan over the years because his hockey career and endorsement deals had kept him in the public eye. And before they'd arrived at the party, Cole had mentioned that his sister, Mia, the youngest, was a designer based in New York, and his middle brother, Rick, traveled the world as a stuntman on movie sets.

"Come on," Cole said. "I'll introduce you."

Marisa bit her lip. "Uh…sure."

The Serenghettis had been a colorful lot so far. She took a deep breath and followed Cole as he made his way toward a lithe and attractive woman who obviously possessed the Serenghetti genes.

"Mia, this is Marisa Danieli."

Cole's sister was beautiful. Her hair was longer than Marisa's, and wavy, not curly. Her almond-shaped eyes tilted slightly upward at the corners, hinting at Slavic or Germanic ancestors—not an uncommon story for those with roots in Italy's north.

"I remember you," Mia said, stepping away from the serving table next to her.

Yikes. In her case and Cole's, recollections of the past couldn't be a good thing. Still, Marisa couldn't fault

Mia if the other woman wanted to size up Cole's newest girlfriend and be protective of her brother. Mia hadn't yet reached high school when she and Cole had been seniors, so Marisa placed her at close to Serafina's age.

Mia tilted her head. "You were the smart girl who brought down the high-and-mighty hockey team captain. Come to finish him off?"

Marisa felt heat flood her cheeks. Still, Mia's tone was surprisingly neutral, joking even. Cole's sister had faulted her brother for his arrogance in high school and called Marisa smart.

"Mia—"

Before Cole could say more, Marisa found her voice. "No, I need him too much to polish him off. He's the headliner for the Pershing fund-raiser." She cast a quick glance at Cole. "Besides, he's shaped up to be a decent guy."

Mia's shoulders relaxed a little. "That's what I think." She smiled. "And you're not his typical fashion-model type."

"Thanks for the endorsement, sis," Cole said drily.

"You could be a model yourself, Mia," Marisa interjected, knowing it wasn't just flattery to get into Mia's good graces, it also happened to be true—Cole's sister was a knockout.

"I was a leg model for a while," Cole's sister admitted, her tone rueful as she pushed one of her chestnut locks over her shoulder. "I didn't like it, but I thought that if I wanted to be a designer, it would help to know the fashion industry from the leg up, if you know what I mean. I did a lot of hosiery ads."

"Yeah," Cole cracked, "I tried to get her to insure her legs."

His tone was jesting but there was also an element of brotherly pride. And Marisa felt a sudden pang at Cole's easy bond with his siblings. She had her cousin Serafina, but they'd always lived in different homes, though sleepovers had made up for some of that distance.

"Hmm," Mia said, considering. "Well, don't count me out on the insurance. I may need to continue to model my own clothes, and from the leg up if it comes to it. Designers starting out have to make do with what they have."

"I've got some helpful advice for you," Cole teased. "Put Jordan in drag. If he's a hit with underwear, he'll rock a strapless dress."

While Marisa smiled at the image, Mia laughed. "Jordan is going to throttle you for suggesting it."

"Don't worry, you've got plenty to hold over him. He'll come cheap."

Marisa warmed to Cole's sister, who obviously had a self-deprecating charm. She could also identify with a woman who was trying to get a career off the ground and running.

Cole looked down at her. "Can I get you a drink?"

"Yes, please," she said, realizing a glass would be a good prop to help disguise her nervousness. "A diet soda would be great."

"I think you need something stronger," Cole teased. "You still haven't met all the Serenghettis."

"I'm going to check in with Mom in the kitchen," Mia announced, stepping back. "Knowing her, she's in a frenzy of activity."

When Cole and Mia had moved off, Marisa found herself alone and looked around. The crowd had thinned—some people heading indoors—and she spotted Serg Serenghetti sitting in a chair near the outdoor kitchen. The family resemblance was unmistakable—she'd have recognized him even if she hadn't seen pictures in the local paper from time to time over the years.

He beckoned to her, and she had no choice but to walk toward him.

Serg's hair was steel-gray mixed with white at the sideburns, and he shared some of his eldest son's features—not to mention Cole's imposing presence, even though he was seated.

When she'd neared, Serg waved a hand to indicate their surroundings. "You're a teacher, Marisa. Based right here in beautiful Welsdale, my wife says. Not like those model types..."

How much had Serg been told about her? "Yes, I've been teaching at the Pershing School since I received my teaching degree. Cole has been generous enough to help with our fund-raiser."

"Pstcha," Serg retorted. "It's not generosity. Cole wants you to keep seeing him."

Marisa had stopped listening at *Cole wants you...*

Serg tilted his head in imitation of his daughter. "Smart guy." Then he adjusted the blanket covering his lap and frowned. "My wife likes to keep me bundled up like an Eskimo facing a blizzard even though spring has come early this year."

Cole returned, drinks in hand. "I see you've met the *pater familias.*" Handing Marisa a wineglass, he added, "He's curmudgeonly in a teddy bear sort of way. I trot him out to make a good impression on the girlfriends."

"Ha!" Serg replied. "I give thanks every day that your fancy schools at least taught you some Latin."

Cole quirked an eyebrow. *"Acta est fabula, plaudita."*

The drama has been acted out, applaud. Marisa hid a smile. She'd studied Latin, too.

"At least I know how to entertain," Serg grumbled. "Smart-ass."

"Chip off the old block."

Serg made some more grousing noises before glancing at Marisa again. "Beautiful woman based right here in Welsdale. Perfect."

"You'd think so," Cole remarked drily.

"Get Marisa to take you on, and you're set. Then you can stay put and run Serenghetti Construction."

"Right."

What? Cole's mocking tone was undeniable but Serg surely couldn't be serious. Marisa felt as if she'd landed in the middle of a family drama that she didn't totally understand.

Serg shook his head. "I had a stroke but I can still understand sarcasm."

"I'm the best you've got. Jordan and Rick are worse."

Camilla appeared and came forward to fuss over her husband, and both Marisa and Cole stepped back.

Serg looked up from under lowered brows. "*Vade in pace.* Go in peace. Latin was required in my day, too, you know."

As she moved aside, Marisa bumped up against something—or rather, someone—and turned around.

A tall, good-looking man smiled down at her. "Hi."

Cole sighed resignedly. "Marisa, this is my brother Rick. The prodigal son back from a film set at the edge of the Earth."

"Don't listen to him," Rick said with a lazy grin. "I'm the movie star. But I've been trying to get Cole here to play one of the bad guys for a long time. With the scars and all, don't you think he looks menacing?"

What Marisa was thinking was that Cole made her heart go pitter-patter...

"You're a stuntman and you've been a body double for Hollywood's A-list," Cole replied. "Still doesn't make you a movie star."

"A fine distinction."

Marisa had to concede that Rick had movie-star looks. Closest in age to Cole, he was also rough-hewn. But he'd been a wrestler, not a hockey player, in high school. That much she knew.

"So word is you two are an item." Rick looked at Cole, his expression droll. "Hot for the teacher?"

Marisa heated to the roots of her hair. She took a sip of wine to fortify herself.

"You can always count on a brother to embarrass you for no reason," Cole said drily, though he didn't look greatly perturbed.

"Your taste in women is improving. What's to be embarrassed about?"

"You."

"Payback." Rick grinned. "So what happened? Marisa clobbered you in high school, and now you're moonstruck?"

Marisa observed the back-and-forth between the brothers, a nervous and self-conscious smile on her lips. Still, it seemed as if Rick was willing to be open-minded about her relationship with his older brother—whatever it was.

Cole, on the other hand, looked as if he was praying for patience. "Mr. Hayes made her 'fess up about who doctored the PowerPoint presentation, smart-ass.

She was going to lose recommendations for a college scholarship."

"No, really," she interjected, "I think that explains my behavior but doesn't excuse it."

"You had a good enough reason for doing what you did," Cole replied.

"I shouldn't have cared about Mr. Hayes's embarrassment." She shrugged. "Chances were good he'd keep his job regardless. You paid a big price."

"I had it coming. Everything worked out eventually."

Marisa wanted to argue further, but then she caught Rick's amused expression.

"What a love-fest," Rick remarked, looking back and forth between them. "I should get out of the way while you two fall all over yourselves making excuses for each other."

Marisa clamped her mouth shut. Something had been changing between her and Cole. She felt as if there were silken ties—a lingerie robe sash came to mind— binding her to him. For his part, Cole seemed as if he couldn't wait to be alone with her again…

Cole linked his hand with hers. "Come on, there are other people I want to introduce you to."

Rick stepped back. "Have fun. I have my hands full avoiding Mom. She wants to capitalize on my rare family appearance."

Murmuring a nice-to-meet-you to Rick, Marisa allowed herself to be led away. Cole introduced her to one group after another until Marisa found it hard to keep track of so many family members, friends and associates. In between, she ate Camilla's delicious food, and Cole had a burger and hot dog while taking his turn grilling.

When they finally reached a lull, Marisa checked her phone and realized they'd already been at the party for three hours.

Cole glanced down at her. "Let's get out of here."

She looked around. "But the party isn't winding down yet."

He gave her a heavy-lidded look. "Right. It's the perfect time to go. People will understand we want to be alone. It'll keep up the appearance that we're a couple."

Nervous anticipation spiraled through her. "Where are we going?"

Taking her hand, Cole raised it to his lips. "My place is closer."

She sucked in a breath. "Okay."

She'd never been in Cole's apartment, and it occurred to her that they were crossing another threshold…

The drive to Cole's was quick. They made their way through the understated lobby and ascended in the elevator to the top floor.

When he let them into his loft, Marisa glanced around. The penthouse was like the home version of Cole's office. Masculine and conveying muted power. Everything looked state-of-the-art—from the electronics that she glimpsed in the living area to the appliances visible in the kitchen.

In the next moment Cole backed her against the exposed brick wall for a searing kiss.

When they broke apart, she said breathlessly, "We have to stop this. We're in a pretend relationship."

"This is helping us pretend better."

"I don't follow your logic."

"Then don't. Just go with the flow."

He was making her feel too much. She was afraid…
and yet she couldn't resist taking the plunge.

He touched her face. "I want to take you on a bed
this time. I want you to cry out my name as I come inside you."

She placed unsteady fingers on the top button of her
shirt, and Cole zeroed in on the action.

"I've been glimpsing your lacy bra all night. The
peekaboo effect has been driving me crazy."

"You've been staring at my breasts?" How many
guests had noticed? And how had she not been aware of
it? Probably because she'd been too nervous and overwhelmed by her surroundings.

"Yeah," Cole said thickly, "and Rick caught me at
it, too. I haven't bumbled so much since high school."

A girlfriend would have told her that her bra was
showing so she could fix the problem. *Not Cole.*

"Think of it as foreplay." He braced a hand on the
wall next to her and leaned in to trail kisses from her
lips to the hollow behind her ear.

She shivered, and her fingers fumbled with the buttons of her shirt. When she finally finished, she tugged
her top out of the waistband of her skirt and opened it
wide. The cool air hit her skin, raising goose bumps.

"So pretty," Cole murmured, trailing a finger from
her jaw, down her neck and to the swell of her breast.

Marisa lowered her eyes as the back of Cole's hand
grazed over the top of her breast…again and again. Her
breath hitched. She couldn't wait to experience what
Cole wanted to show her—and do with her—this time.

He slid one hand up her thigh and under her skirt,
and she leaned against the wall for support. He nuzzled

her neck, and then found her with his hand, delving inside her welcoming moistness.

She tangled her hands in his hair. "Cole."

"Yeah?" he said thickly.

"Tell me this isn't in the playbook."

"No, but this is." He crouched and moments later used his tongue at her most sensitive spot.

Her knees nearly buckled, and she sank her fingers into his hair, anchoring herself in a world flooded with sensation. "Cole, please."

"Please, what?" he muttered. "Keep going?"

She was so aroused that she couldn't breathe right. "Oh…"

"My pleasure."

Minutes later her world splintered, coming apart like a kaleidoscope exploding, and she sagged against the wall.

Cole straightened, bracing himself with a hand against the wall near her face, his eyes glittering.

"You're going to ride me," he said huskily. "You're breasts are going to bounce and drive me crazy…and then after you scream for me, I'm going to come inside you in one long rush."

Marisa parted her lips. She'd never been so turned on in her life.

"Bed. Now," she gasped.

"The magic words," he responded, grinning.

He swung her into his arms and strode down the hall. The bedroom was at the end, on the right.

It was an enormous room, with skylights and glass doors opening onto a terrace.

When he set her feet down, they both stripped, their fingers working quickly on more buttons. He beat her to the finish—naked when she still had on a bra and panties.

He prowled toward her with purpose. *He was perfect.* All muscle and sculpted maleness. Not an ounce of softness, but still, she was prepared to be cosseted.

He cupped her breasts, kissed the top of each one and then claimed her mouth. With a deft move, he undid her bra and she spilled against him.

He pushed down her panties until they pooled at her feet. And then he was laying her down on the bed and stretching over her. He fanned her hair out across the pillow.

"What are you doing?"

He gave her a crooked smile. "This is the way I've fantasized about you. Your hair spread across my bed... entangling me."

"I thought I was going to be on top."

"You will be," he promised before he kissed his way down her body.

When he was ready, he flipped her on top of him.

She straddled him, and then sank onto him until they were joined. They both groaned, and he helped her set up a rhythm that they enjoyed.

When she finally crested on a wave that was pure and beautiful, she heard her own gasps of pleasure as if from a distant place. Cole's face was contorted with effort until he found his own release and spilled inside her in one long thrust.

Marisa sagged forward against him, and he caught her, their hearts racing.

"I don't think I can survive much more of you, Marisa."

"You don't need to," she murmured. "I've given you all I have."

It was true—and also what she was afraid of. Cole had her body and soul. She only hoped she wasn't just another score...

"Cole, come on up and taste Marisa's cooking."

Cole smiled for the camera. Which producer had come up with this stunt? Or had it been his mother's idea? His mother was looking excited and decidedly innocent. Never mind that the dish to be sampled had more accurately been a joint production of Marisa *and* both their mothers.

If Marisa hadn't been looking so horrified—but how many of her students tuned in to local television in the middle of the afternoon?—he might have suspected her of having a hand in the making of this made-for-TV moment. As it was, he wanted to laugh. He hadn't expected to be an extra in this episode of his mother's show.

When he reached the stage, he said gamely, "I'm sure it's delicious, but I'm not a connoisseur."

Camilla gave Marisa a spoon with a sampling of *tiella* on it—bits of rice, onion, potato and mussels mixed together—and nodded expectantly.

When Marisa turned, she made to hand off the spoon to him.

"No, no, Marisa," Camilla said laughingly. "I always raise the spoon to the *bocca* when I ask my family for an *opinione*."

The audience laughed along gamely, and even Donna smiled at Camilla's exuberant admonishment.

Cole could read the defeat in Marisa's eyes as she realized there was no way out. Unlike him, she wasn't

used to being on camera. But they both knew everyone—the audience, their mothers and the producers—
was waiting for her to feed him.

Slowly, she raised the spoon, cupping her other hand
under it to prevent spills. He locked his gaze on her
face, and at the last second, took hold of her wrist in
order to guide it. She gasped softly, the moment between them becoming molten even before the food
touched his mouth.

The seafood dish was delicious. She was delicious.
He wanted to start with the *tiella* and then have his fill
of her until he was satisfied—though he had no idea
when that would be. He'd always thought she was edible, but a taste wasn't enough. Their two trysts had just
whetted his appetite. He wished he could say he was
sorry for roping her into an appearance on his mother's
show, but the truth was he looked forward to any opportunity to be around her these days.

Marisa finally pulled away, lowering the spoon and
looking flustered.

Camilla clapped, her expression expectant. "So?"

Cole swallowed and cleared his throat, raising his
gaze from Marisa. "Mmm…fantastic. You could tell it
was prepared with love."

He didn't know where he was dredging up the words.
He figured he was having an out-of-body experience
since he couldn't ever remember being this turned on
without having a blatant physical sign of arousal—
which would have been an inconvenient turn of events
right now, to say the least, even with a kitchen counter
providing camouflage from the cameras.

His mother turned to address the audience, saving
him from the spotlight. "And now for another special

surprise. We are giving away a set of Stanhope Department Store's own brand of stainless-steel cookware today, thanks to our guest, Donna Casale. You can try yourself today's recipe with your own new cookware!"

To much applause, a producer lifted the top of a big, white box to reveal a ten-piece set of gleaming stainless-steel pots and pans.

"Please look under your seats!" Camilla announced. "The person with the red dot is the winner!"

After a few moments, a middle-aged woman stood up excitedly and waved a disc.

"Auguri!" Camilla called, clapping. "Come down to look at your gift."

When the audience member arrived to inspect her prize, Camilla put an arm around her and turned to the camera. "If you like the Danieli family recipe, please go to our website."

She paused for what Cole knew would be a voice-over, and the appearance onscreen of the recipe and web address when the episode aired. Then Camilla thanked her guests and the audience members for coming. "Until next time. *Alla salute!*"

When the camera lights turned off, signaling the end of filming, Marisa visibly relaxed.

"Good job, Mom," Cole said.

Camilla gave him a beatific smile. "Thank you for *l'assistenza.*"

If he wasn't saving one parent, he was saving another. Though he doubted his father would think Cole was saving anything when he heard there was finally a buyer interested in Serenghetti Construction. He'd received an offer earlier in the week but hadn't shared the news yet with anyone.

At the moment, though, he had more pressing concerns. As the audience began to rise and disperse, he cupped Marisa's elbow.

"Are you okay?" he asked in a low voice. "You looked as if you were about to have a swoon-worthy moment back there."

"Only for your legion of female fans," she replied, blowing a stray hair away from her face.

He suppressed a laugh. *That'a girl.*

His mother and Donna were approached by a couple of audience members, so he and Marisa had relative privacy.

"Looks as if you might have gained some admirers today, too," he remarked.

She eyed him. "Including you?"

"I've always been a fan."

"Of my cooking?"

"Of everything, sweet pea."

Marisa waved a hand in front of her face. "You do know how to turn up the heat."

He gave her an intimate smile. "We haven't done it in the kitchen yet."

At her wide-eyed look, he bit back a grin. He admitted it—he loved flustering Marisa.

"There are other people here," she replied in a low, urgent voice.

He leaned over to whisper in her ear. "Your kitchen or mine?"

She sucked in a breath. "I—I have to show out my mom."

He gave her a lingering look, but nodded. Sooner or later, he'd have another chance to fan the flames with

Marisa. He figured he'd survived the last fifteen years only because he hadn't known what he'd been missing...

As Marisa walked out of the television studio with her mother toward the exit that led to the parking lot, she kept her thoughts to herself.

"So what am I not supposed to know?" Donna asked lightly.

Marisa threw her a sidelong look. "I don't know what you mean."

"Hmm...it looks like it's more than just business between you and Cole Serenghetti."

Marisa felt a telltale wave of heat rise to her face. "Just doing a favor to thank him for participating in the fund-raiser," she mumbled. "Besides, I thought it would be fun. You love cooking shows. Didn't you have fun?"

"Yes, I did," Donna agreed, "and part of it was the enjoyment of watching you and Cole interact. He looked as if he couldn't wait to be alone with you."

"Mom!"

Donna turned to face her. "You're a beautiful, desirable woman, Marisa. I know what a prize my daughter is. Cole would be foolish not to be interested in you."

There was the problem in a nutshell. She wasn't sure where she and Cole stood—where pretending left off and reality began. And whether they were just hooking up with no possibility of a future together.

"Camilla Serenghetti, for one, believes something is going on, and she couldn't be happier about it. She said she's heard rumors around town..." Donna sighed and then gave her a long-suffering look. "The mothers are always the last to know."

Marisa sighed herself, not having the heart for further denials. "Cole and I have a complicated past."

"All relationships are complicated, honey. But what I saw in there was Cole eating you up with his eyes."

"Mom, please!" she protested, because she wasn't used to such frank talk from her mother.

Donna laughed. "Honey, I'm acquainted with the attractiveness of pro athletes."

"Of course you are."

Her mother looked at her probingly. "I hope your hesitancy about Cole doesn't have anything to do with what happened between me and your father."

They stopped at the closed door leading out of the building.

When Marisa didn't say anything, Donna added, "Oh, honey, if baseball hadn't broken us up, something else would have. We were too young."

Yup, Marisa could identify with the tragedy of young love. She and Cole had been there themselves.

Still, she was surprised by her mother's toned-down reaction. Ever since Marisa had discovered the truth in her twenties about her parents' relationship—that her biological father was out of the picture even before an accident had claimed his life—she'd assumed her mother would be averse to professional athletes and their lifestyle.

Sure, her mother had been matter-of-fact when she'd finally detailed the circumstances around her pregnancy, but Marisa had assumed her mother had adopted that attitude for her daughter's sake. Marisa had vivid memories of exactly what sacrifices had been involved in her upbringing, and she figured her mother did, too, and despite hiding it well, couldn't help but be infected with some bitterness.

It appeared she was wrong—at least these days.

"You know, Mom," Marisa said jokingly, "marriage really has changed your outlook on life."

"Older and wiser, honey," Donna replied. "But the events in my life that you're referring to also happened a long time ago. I had time to move past them and get on with it. And I have never, ever regretted having you. You were a gift."

Tears sprung to Marisa's eyes. "Oh, Mom, stop."

Donna gave her a quick squeeze and then laughed lightly. "Enough about Cole Serenghetti, you mean? Well, let me know what happens there. Sometimes mothers would like to move up from last on the totem pole!"

Ten

Marisa looked around the glittering ballroom where the Pershing Shines Bright fund-raiser was being held. The Briarcliff was a popular event venue on the outskirts of Welsdale. It was also one of the locations she'd scouted for her wedding to Sal.

That last thought made her realize how much had changed—how much *she'd* changed—in the past several months. The man uppermost in her mind was Cole, not Sal.

Because tonight was bittersweet. She was relieved the fund-raiser had come together as a nice event. Thanks to Cole, they'd sold more tickets than she'd ever hoped for, and Jordan was a hit, as well. But even though she and Cole had not talked further about it, after this evening they were scheduled to drop their charade about being a couple.

She looked across the room at where Cole stood talking to Mr. Dobson, and her heart squeezed.

Cole looked beyond handsome in a tux. She knew he'd have no trouble attracting female interest again once people no longer thought that he was dating her. In fact, more than one woman tonight had thrown him an appreciative look or had hung on his words and giggled at something he'd said.

Marisa sighed. She should be focused on other things. Her mother and stepfather were here to support her. And after this evening, she might have proved herself enough to become assistant principal at Pershing. Mr. Dobson had asked her last week to submit her résumé.

The principal had given no indication that he was aware of her relationship with Cole—and she certainly hadn't broadcast it at school. In fairness, however, she'd casually mentioned that she and Cole had begun to see each other, having become reacquainted over preparations for Pershing Shines Bright. Marisa figured it was best the principal got the news from her first. And if Mr. Dobson had been a fan of *Flavors of Italy with Camilla Serenghetti*, he would have seen the episode with her and Cole that had aired two weeks ago, a few days after taping.

Cole glanced her way, and their gazes locked, his look appreciative.

He made her feel beautiful. She wore a green satin dress with a black lace overlay covering the sweetheart neckline, and chandelier earrings. She'd chosen her outfit with him in mind.

In the past couple of weeks, she'd seen more of Cole than she would ever have imagined. They'd attended a

Razors game together to cheer on Jordan, where they were even nabbed on the Jumbotron sharing a quick kiss. She'd attended his second hockey clinic for Pershing students, and she'd teased him about making a teacher out of him yet. They'd also bonded in the kitchen, where he'd helped her make some of her signature Italian dishes.

She heated at the thought of what else they'd recently done in the kitchen...

Marisa had known then, if she hadn't before, that she'd fallen in love with him. Because heartbreak was her middle name.

"My God, he only has eyes for you."

Marisa jumped, yanked from her reverie, and turned to see Serafina behind her. "You sound like a bad advertisement for a women's hair-care product."

Serafina shook her head. "It's not your hair that I'm talking about."

"Ladies."

She and Serafina swung in unison to see Cole's youngest brother.

Jordan's eyes came to rest on Serafina, and his smile was enough to melt ice. "Marisa didn't tell me she had an even more perfect relative."

"Oh?" Serafina responded and then glanced behind her. "Where is she?"

Cole's brother grinned. "I'm looking at her, angel. I'm—"

Serafina scowled. "My name is not Angel, and I know who you are."

"Cole's brother," Jordan supplied, still unperturbed.

"The New England Razors' right wingman and leading scorer."

Jordan's smile remained in place. "You watch hockey."

"Leading scorer on and off the field," Serafina elaborated, her voice cool. "I read the news, too. And I've been moonlighting as a waitress at the Puck & Shoot."

"I know, and yet somehow we've never been introduced."

"Fortunately."

Marisa cleared her throat. She was happy she was no longer the focus of Sera's attention, but it was time to step in. "Jordan, this is my cousin Serafina."

"Named for the angels," Jordan murmured. "I was right. Must be divine kismet."

"In your dreams."

"It's where you'll be tonight…unless you also want to join me at the bar later?"

"My God, don't you stop?"

Marisa knew Serafina didn't like players, but she'd never known her cousin to be rude.

Sera's scowl deepened. "How did you know Marisa and I were related?"

For the first time, Jordan's gaze left Serafina for a moment. "Same delicate bone structure, and smooth cocoa butter skin. What's to mistake?"

"Unfortunately nothing, I suppose," Serafina allowed reluctantly.

"You're lovely."

"You're persistent."

"Part of my charm."

"Debatable."

Jordan grinned again and then shrugged. "The offer still stands. The bar, later."

"You're going to be lonely," Serafina replied. "At least for my company."

Jordan kept his easy expression as he stepped away. "Nice to meet you…Angel."

Serafina waited until Jordan was out of earshot and then fixed Marisa with a look. "A professional player."

"Cole is one, too."

"He's retired from the game. At least the one on the ice."

And then with a huff, her cousin turned and marched off, leaving Marisa speechless.

Cole appeared next to her. "What happened?"

She shook her head. "Actually, I don't know, except your brother and my cousin did not hit it off."

Cole frowned. "Surprising. Jordan is usually able to charm the—"

"—panties off any woman?" she finished bluntly for him.

Cole smiled ruefully.

"I think that's Serafina's issue with him."

Cole leaned in close, nuzzling Marisa's hairline. "The only woman I want to use my charm on is you."

Marisa's pulse sped up. "We can't here."

"We're supposed to be a couple."

One that would soon be *uncoupled*. "We're supposed to be professional, too."

She looked away, and then froze as she spotted a familiar figure across the room.

Cole's brows drew together. "What's wrong?"

He followed her gaze, and then he stilled, too.

Mr. Hayes. The former principal had been invited tonight because he usually was for major school events. She just hadn't thought of apprising Cole of the fact. And she'd sort of ducked the issue by not checking with the administrative staff about whether Mr. Hayes had said he would be attending.

She hoped a meeting fifteen years in the making wouldn't spell disaster...

"Cole Serenghetti and Marisa Danieli," Mr. Hayes hailed them.

Cole looked at Marisa but she was avoiding his eyes.

"Mr. Hayes," she greeted the other man. "How nice to see you. You look wonderful. Retirement agrees with you."

Retirement would have agreed with the sour Mr. Hayes fifteen years ago, Cole thought sardonically. Of course, the old codger would be here tonight. He was grayer and less imposing than when he'd held Cole's fate in his hands, but he still had the same ponderous personality from the looks of it.

Cole gazed at Marisa, and she implored him with her eyes to make nice. Tonight was important to her, so he was willing to go along. He gave her a slow smile. *You owe me, and I'll collect later, in a mutually pleasurable way...*

Mr. Hayes glanced from Cole to Marisa. "I understand you two are a couple these days. Congratulations."

Marisa smiled. "Thank you."

"I bet you're surprised," Cole put in.

Marisa appeared as if she wanted to give him a sharp elbow.

"Not really," Mr. Hayes replied.

Cole arched an eyebrow. "I turned out better than you expected."

"Well, naturally—"

"I understand there'll be a video retrospective tonight. Might want to withhold judgment until then."

Marisa widened her eyes at him, and Cole smiled insouciantly back at her. He was willing to play along, but he could still tweak Mr. Hayes's nose and have some fun in the process.

Mr. Hayes cleared his throat. "Speaking of video presentations, I would like to set the record straight on one issue. When Marisa was called to my office that day, and I asked—"

"Interrogated, you mean?"

"—her about the prank, I could tell she cared about you."

Cole tamped down his surprise.

"At first, she was very reluctant to say anything. And then when she revealed your connection to the stunt, she was worried about what would happen to you."

Cole felt Marisa's touch on his arm.

She'd cared about him in high school, and even Mr. Hayes had been able to see it. Cole wondered why he himself hadn't, and realized it was because he'd been blind to anything but his sense of betrayal.

Cole met and held Mr. Hayes's gaze. "I learned a lot from that episode in high school. It was the last school prank I ever pulled." He covered Marisa's hand with his. "But everything ended well. More than fine. I'm lucky."

Marisa went still, and Cole figured she was wondering whether he was playacting for Mr. Hayes's benefit. She probably thought he was highlighting their relationship in order to rub the former principal's nose in it.

But he wasn't acting. He was dead serious. The realization hit him like a body check on the ice.

He wanted Marisa in his life. He *needed her* in his life.

Sooner or later, he was going to make her see she needed him, too.

Two days after the fund-raiser Marisa opened her door to the last person she expected to catch on her threshold again. Sal.

Since Pershing Shines Bright, she hadn't had a chance to see Cole again, though he'd congratulated her by text on a job well done. She'd been on duty the night of the fund-raiser, so she'd departed after everyone but Pershing staff had left. After a quick peck on the lips, Cole had regretfully excused himself because he had an early-morning work meeting.

She was left in a crazy-making limbo about where she and Cole stood, wondering whether the meeting was an excuse because he remembered, too, that the clock on their relationship was due to strike midnight at the end of the fund-raiser.

Still, the morning—or two—after, she hadn't expected Sal.

She reluctantly stepped aside so he could make it over the threshold. "Sal."

"Marisa, I need to talk to you."

Closing the door, she turned to face her former fiancé.

"Vicki left me," Sal said without preamble.

"I'm sorry."

Well, this was an interesting turn of events. Marisa wrapped her arms around herself. In some ways, she should have predicted Sal and Vicki's breakup. They appeared to have little in common, except perhaps for their joint affinity for sports stars.

Still, what did Sal want from her? A shoulder to cry on? She needed consoling herself about Cole.

Sal grimaced. "It was for the best that Vicki made for the door. I've been acting like an idiot."

Marisa couldn't disagree, but she said nothing, not wanting to hit someone when he was down.

Sal suddenly looked at her pleadingly. "I'm done with the high-flying lifestyle of pro athletes, Marisa. I thought I wanted it for myself, but I've tendered my resignation at the sports agency. I'm taking a job with a foundation that brings sports and athletics to underprivileged kids. I want to make a difference."

She couldn't argue with the admirable impulse to help kids. She worked with children every day. It was exhausting but exhilarating work. Still, while she was happy Sal appeared to be in a better place, she wondered about the road he'd taken to get there. "And Vicki leaving you led to this epiphany?"

He had the grace to look sheepish. "She wasn't you, Marisa."

"Of course not. Wasn't that why you were attracted to her?"

"I was an idiot," Sal repeated. "But I've done a lot of thinking in the past few days."

She waited.

"Marisa, I still have feelings for you."

She blinked and dropped her arms to her sides.

Sal held up his hand. "Wait, let me finish. I know it'll be hard to regain your trust. But I hope it won't be impossible. I'm asking you to give me another chance." He reached for her hand. "Marisa, I love you. I'm willing to do anything, whatever it takes, to have you back."

She didn't know where to begin. "Sal—"

"You don't need to say anything." Sal gave a half laugh. "There's nothing you can say that I haven't already thought of. I've called myself every name in the book."

She snapped her mouth closed.

"The thing is, I got cold feet with our engagement." He shrugged. "You could say it took Vicki to make me realize the person I really want. You, Marisa."

As a heartfelt declaration, it wasn't half-bad. But she was no longer sure he was the right man for her.

Sal had made a mistake, by his own admission. But otherwise he was safe and predictable and what she'd thought she always wanted—until Cole had come back into her life.

Still, Cole had never shown any indication of settling down. And while she'd been falling in love with him, he hadn't given any sign that he returned her feelings.

She cleared her throat. "Sal, I—"

"No," he interrupted. "Don't say anything. Think about it. I know I've laid a lot on you."

"Really—"

He gave her a quick kiss, startling her. It was as if he was determined to prevent a knee-jerk rejection. "I'm going to check in with you again soon."

With those words, Sal turned and was out the door as quickly as he had come.

Cole had just gotten off a conference call at work when his assistant put through a call from Steve Fryer, an acquaintance from his days on the ice.

Cole looked at the papers strewn across his desk. He was already pressed for time, his morning occupied with meetings, but Steve had no way of knowing that.

Cole also itched to be with Marisa. He hadn't seen her since the fund-raiser a few days ago. He'd had a busy schedule with a couple of work emergencies, and today was looking no better.

"Cole, I've got good news," Steve announced. "The coach for the Madison Rockets has decided to take the job in Canada after all because the sports advertising agency there agreed to meet his contract terms." Pause. "We'd like to offer you the coaching position."

Cole leaned back in his chair, his world coming to a screeching halt. This was the opportunity he'd been waiting months for. The Rockets were one of the best minor league teams in the American Hockey League. The job would be a good launching pad for an NHL coaching position. Rather than starting as an assistant coach in the NHL, he could prove himself as the head of his own team.

"Great news, Steve. I think the Rockets made the right decision."

Steve laughed.

"I'll get back to you," Cole said, eyeing the jumble of papers on his desk. "As you can imagine, there are things to sort out at this end." He expected Steve would assume he needed to contact his agent—or former agent, to be more accurate—to begin the process of negotiating a suitable employment contract.

Only Cole knew his complications were bigger. He needed to disentangle himself from Serenghetti Construction, for one. He thought again of the offer to purchase the company—it was now or never. And then there was his relationship with Marisa...

"Take your time," Steve responded. "We'll talk next week."

"You'll be hearing from me." Cole gave the assurance before ending the call, his mind buzzing.

The wheels were moving in the direction he wanted, but in the past year he'd become more encumbered than ever in Welsdale. Marisa was chief among those ties...

He'd suggest she move to Madison with him.

A weight lifted as his mind sped up. There would be plenty of teaching jobs there for her. If she had the potential to advance at Pershing, then she certainly had the qualifications to be an attractive hire at other schools. She might even decide that moving someplace else was the better bet—she hadn't yet gotten a promotion at Pershing, and one might never materialize. Another school might start her out in administration from the beginning.

He could make this situation work—for the both of them. He *would* make it work.

But first he needed to tackle a dicier situation. It was time to tell Serg about the offer to buy Serenghetti Construction.

Cole picked up his jacket off the back of the chair and told the receptionist he'd be out and reachable on his cell. After texting his mother, he made the quick drive over to Casa Serenghetti, where he figured he'd find Serg in one of two moods: grumpy or grumpier.

When he stepped inside the house, he greeted his mother with a peck on the cheek and then followed her to the oversize family room, where his father was ensconced in a club chair.

Cole sat in a leather chair and braced his elbows on his knees, his hands clasped between them. Camilla took a seat on the sofa, and there was small talk about the weather and how Serg was feeling. But Cole could tell his father was suspicious about this unexpected visit. Serg regarded him from under his customary lowered brows.

Cole took the bull by the horns. "Someone's offered to buy the company."

"Offered?" Serg shot back in his rumbling voice. "Like someone came banging on your door? Or you solicited a buyer?"

"Does it matter? It's a good offer from a bigger outfit with operations in the Northeast." Cole knew they couldn't expect better.

Serg grumbled, his eyes piercing. "I'm going to have another stroke." Then he bent his head and grimaced.

Camilla shot to her feet. "Madonna. Serg! Where does it hurt?"

But Cole had a better question. "Right now?"

Serg cracked one eye open. "Does it matter when? You've killed me, either way."

"Serg, please," Camilla exclaimed, throwing Cole an exasperated look.

Cole was used to drama from his family. He'd had a lifetime of it.

"You fought hard to get the contract to build the Pershing gym, and now you're planning to sell the company?" Serg asked accusingly. "I was starting to think you had my competitive business instincts."

Cole was ready. "I do, and that's why I believe selling the company is the best thing."

"Camilla, bring me my meds," Serg instructed at the same time that he waved Cole away. "I need to rest."

"The offer is a good one," Cole said again, and then stood because he'd known before he'd arrived that he needed to let Serg get used to the idea. "Let me know when you're ready to hear more of the particulars."

One meeting down, one to go. On the way out the door, Cole texted Marisa to meet him at the Puck & Shoot after work…

Eleven

When Marisa walked into the Puck & Shoot, she was nervous. Cole had asked her to meet him, and she knew she needed to mention Sal's visit.

She slipped into the booth and sat opposite from Cole, not giving him a chance to rise at her entrance. A waitress appeared, and at Cole's inquiring look, she ordered a light beer.

Cole's cell phone buzzed, and she was saved from having to say anything more. Apologizing for having to take a work call, he stood up and walked a few feet away.

The last time she and Cole had been at the Puck & Shoot, she'd thrown herself at him when Sal and Vicki had appeared, and their charade as a couple had started. How fitting would it be if they buried their faux relationship here, as well?

When the waitress returned and set her drink before her, Marisa took a swallow. She was nervous, and she sensed something was up with Cole, too.

Cole slipped back into the booth, pocketing his phone.

Marisa felt her pulse pick up. She wanted to slide into the booth beside him, sit in his lap, twine her arms around his neck and brush his lips with hers. But she no longer knew whether she was allowed to. She didn't know where they stood. Neither of them had talked about anything substantial since the end of the fundraiser days ago.

As if reading her mind, Cole stared at her intently. "We've done a good job pretending to be a couple."

"Yes." It was the pretend part that she'd had trouble with.

"I've been offered a coaching job with a hockey team in Madison, Wisconsin."

Marisa's heart plummeted.

Cole, however, looked pleased. Could their relationship—okay, their pretending—have meant so little to him? She wondered why he'd brought up the coaching job right after mentioning their charade. It seemed like a non sequitur...unless this was Cole's way of breaking things off? *It's been good, but now I'm moving on, sweet pea?*

"Sal wants to get back together," she blurted.

She knew it was a defensive move, but she couldn't help herself. Cole hadn't said he was taking the job in Wisconsin, but...he seemed happy. And he knew she was tied to Welsdale and her job at Pershing School—not that he'd said anything about having her move with him.

Her mind was racing, but she just couldn't bear to hear the words *it's over, baby.* She'd been dumped by Sal and had survived, but she wasn't sure she could pick up the pieces after Cole. He meant too much. Still, she couldn't blame Cole for leaving. The fund-raiser was finished, and she'd been the one to insist their pretend relationship would end with it.

Cole blinked, and then his face tightened. "Don't tell me you're considering giving that jerk a second chance."

No, but right now she needed her walls up where Cole was concerned. She had to keep him at a distance. She'd fallen in love with him, but he'd never given any indication that he felt the same way about her. In fact, he was leaving.

Cole nodded curtly. "If you go back to Sal, you'll be playing it safe."

"I'm a teacher. It's a nice, safe profession."

He leaned forward. "If you think you're not passionate and daring, you're wrong, sweet pea. I can tell after our time together."

She wasn't passionate, she was greedy. She wanted it all, including Cole's unwavering love and attention. But Cole had never shown any inclination of settling down, and as far as she could tell, he wasn't starting now. "You're passionate about hockey. You should pursue the dream."

It hurt to say the words. She felt a heavy weight lodge in her heart. But if there was one thing she'd learned from the past, it was that it was futile to stand in the way of dreams.

Cole said nothing, but his hand tightened on his beer.

"Sure your parents would love to have you in Welsdale," she continued. "That's why they liked that we were a couple. But we both know it was pretend." Just saying those words made her ill.

Cole's mouth thinned. "Are you forgetting how we got into a fake relationship?"

Yes, it was her fault. She heated but stood her ground. "And now we're uncoupled."

He gave a brief nod. "There's nothing else to say then. A bargain is a bargain."

Marisa wanted to say a lot of things. *I love you. Don't leave. Stay with me.*

Instead, she nodded in agreement and reached for her handbag beside her. She fumbled for bills to pay her tab.

"Leave it," Cole said, his voice and face impassive. "I've got it."

She nodded and slid out of the booth without looking at him. "I've got to go. I squeezed in a detour to the Puck & Shoot when you texted, but I've got papers to grade tonight."

She would not meet Cole's gaze. It would be her undoing. "Thanks for the beer."

She headed toward the door on autopilot. *Please don't let me faint. Please let me survive this.*

The next night Cole found himself at the Puck & Shoot again. Anyone with a morbid sense of humor would say he enjoyed wallowing in misery by returning to the scene of the crime.

He still knew which way was up, but he hoped to correct the situation soon, starting with the drink before him. He'd never been turned this inside out by a breakup with a woman, and it took some getting used to.

On top of it, he was questioning his plans for Serenghetti Construction. If that wasn't evidence that he needed his head examined, he didn't know what was. Without his knowing it, the family company had grown on him in a sneaky way. It didn't seem right to sell it.

He grimaced. He could handle only one breakup at a time.

"What are you doing? Drinking yourself silly?"

Cole turned, surprised at his brother's voice. "Your powers of observation are impressive, Jordan."

Cole figured he should have chosen a bar other than the Puck & Shoot if he'd wanted to be left alone. At least Marisa's cousin Serafina wasn't working tonight. Unfortunately, however, Jordan had decided to show up for a drink.

"Well? Where's Marisa?" Jordan looked around the bar. "It's Saturday night. I thought you two lovebirds were joined at the beak these days."

"She decided she prefers another guy."

Jordan raised his eyebrows. "Sal?"

Cole didn't answer.

"And you're conceding the field?"

"She made her choice," he responded.

Jordan shook his head. "Man, you are pathetic—"

Cole grabbed a fistful of his brother's shirt and got in Jordan's face. "Leave it alone." Then he thrust his brother away and took another swallow of his scotch. He needed something stronger than a beer tonight.

"You can't see what's in front of your eyes."

Cole propped a hand up in front of him on the bar and spread his fingers. "I'm not that far gone. Yet."

"You want her bad."

"There are other women."

"Vicki."

"Hell, no. We're through."

"So you aren't willing to settle for any—"

"She is." He didn't need to elaborate who the *she* was. *Marisa*. She'd been in his thoughts nonstop. "She's willing to take the horn-dog back."

"Has she said so?"

"She's considering it."

Jordan looked around. "I thought she'd be here."

"Why the hell would she be here?"

"She texted me earlier. She's looking for you. She said she had something of yours to return—"

Probably his heart.

"—and I told her I had no idea where you were, but the Puck & Shoot was worth a try."

Great. There was no way he wanted his brother—and who knew how many others—to witness his final denouement. "She knows how to break up with a guy."

"Too public?" Jordan guessed. "Why don't you go to her apartment then and beat her to it?"

Brilliant idea. The last thing he needed was for Marisa to find him at the Puck & Shoot, nursing a drink like a lonely lovesick puppy. If he seemed pathetic to Jordan, he didn't want to think how he'd appear to Marisa.

If she was looking for him, best to get this over with. He'd save her the hassle of finding him. At least that was what he told himself. He ignored the way his pulse picked up at the thought of seeing her again.

Cole straightened off the bar stool and tossed some bills on the counter for the waiter.

"I'll get you a cab," Jordan offered.

Cole twisted his lips. "Because I'm not fit to drive?"

"Because you're not fit for public consumption. You

look like hell, and something tells me you were that way even before you got to the Puck & Shoot."

The ride to Marisa's apartment was swift.

When Cole reached Marisa's door, it was open a crack. He heard voices and pushed his way inside without invitation.

The scene that greeted him made his blood boil. At the entrance to the living room, Sal and Marisa were locked in a tight embrace, Sal's lips diving for hers. It would have been an arresting tableau even without his appearance as the spurned ex-lover, Cole thought, but his unexpected arrival had turned this into a spectator sport.

"Sal, no!" Marisa tried to shrug out of Piazza's grasp.

The scene before him took on an entirely new cast. Cole sprang forward and yanked Sal away, shoving him up against the wall. He put his face in the sports agent's surprised one.

"She said no," he said between clenched teeth.

"Hey, man…"

Cole gave Piazza a rough shake. "Understand?"

"We were just—"

He slammed the other guy back against the wall. "You were just leaving."

Sal struggled. "Get off me. I have every right to visit my girlfriend."

"Your former girlfriend," Cole corrected.

"Same goes," Sal retorted. "You sports guys think you can have whatever you like whenever you want it. How does it feel to be dumped for a change?"

Cole glanced over at Marisa. He was at a disadvantage because he didn't know what she had said to Sal and what she hadn't.

She looked at him mutely for an instant, as if dumbfounded, and then stepped closer. "Cole, don't hurt him."

Cole turned back to Sal, staring down the red-faced sports agent.

"I'll sue you," Sal said.

"That's what it's always been about," Cole said. "You hankered for the money and the women, and the other baggage that comes with a pro athlete's life. Is that why you want Marisa back, too?"

Marisa gasped.

Sal gave a disbelieving laugh. "I've wised up. You're on an ego trip, Serenghetti."

"Not as big as the one you're on, Piazza."

Marisa came closer. "Cole, let him go. Sal, you need to leave now."

The threat of violence hung in the air even as Cole dropped his hold and stepped back.

Sal shrugged and straightened his collar. Then he ran his hand through his hair before settling his gaze on Marisa. "You know where to reach me, honey. I'll leave you to give Serenghetti his walking papers. He must have had trouble reading them the first time."

Cole tightened his hand into a fist, but he let the sports agent make his exit without further incident.

When the door to the apartment clicked shut, Marisa turned toward Cole. It was quiet, and they both seemed to realize at the same time that they were now alone to face the charged emotions between them.

"What are you doing here?" Marisa asked.

"Thank you, Cole, for saving me," he replied in a falsetto voice.

"I can take care of myself."

"Right." He still wanted to break Sal in two. "Here's the better question. What was Sal doing here, and if he wants you to take him back, why were you resisting?"

"Sal and I aren't back together."

Despite himself, Cole felt better. She hadn't taken Sal back *yet*, and from the looks of things, Sal may just have ruined his chances.

"But I told him the reason wasn't because you and I are still together."

"So he saw his opportunity to press his case?"

Marisa sucked in a breath. "Next question. Why did you show up? You couldn't have known Sal was here."

"Jordan said you were trying to track me down."

She shook her head. "No."

Cole clenched his fist. Either his brother was misinformed, or Jordan had duped him into going to Marisa's apartment. If he hadn't agreed to go, would Jordan have tried to lure Marisa down to the Puck & Shoot instead? One thing was for sure—he was going to do physical violence to his brother, upcoming hockey playoffs or no.

First, though, he needed to get one thing straight. "Fine, you weren't trying to track me down. I've still got something to say."

Marisa stared at him without saying a word.

"You're a beautiful woman. You're ambitious and passionate and worthy of whatever life throws at you. The two of us might be finished, but don't settle for Sal."

He wanted to grab her and kiss her, but that would

put him in Piazza's league. Instead, he forced himself to turn and walk out the door.

Marisa expected the senior play to be the last big event on the school calendar at Pershing. She didn't think, though, that the seniors' swan song would also be the place she ran into Cole again—maybe for the last time before he left Welsdale.

Ever since he'd left her apartment last week, she'd been thinking about him. She wasn't about to take Sal back just because Cole intended to leave town for a coaching job in another state. Sal had only been a convenient smokescreen when Cole had announced he was moving to Wisconsin—and yet the realization that Cole may have been misled had done nothing to ease her heartache...

She also had no idea why Jordan would have told Cole that she was looking for him. Maybe Jordan had been misinformed—or maybe he was trying to get the two of them back together. No, the latter was wishful thinking.

She stole a look at Cole, who was sitting across the aisle in a different section of the auditorium. Would she ever stop yearning where he was concerned? She assumed Cole had been invited to the play by Mr. Dobson because he was a famous alumnus intertwined with the school's plans for the future.

Even with the space separating her and Cole, however, she had trouble concentrating. Even more depressingly, Pershing's seniors were staging *Death of a Salesman*. And as the scene opened, her heart rose to her throat. Because there it was...

The sofa where she had lost her virginity to Cole.

Right there on stage. She burned to the roots of her hair. She stared ahead, not daring a glance at Cole. Out of the periphery of her eye, however, she thought she detected a movement of his head in her direction...

Marisa didn't know how she made it through the rest of the play. The sofa...the memories...Cole. She longed to race up the aisle, through the doors to the auditorium and all the way home...where she could console herself in private.

She loved Cole, and he didn't love her in return. It was a replay of high school. And like her mother, she was getting burned by a pro athlete who wanted to pursue his dreams.

Somehow she made it through the whole play. She breathed a sigh of relief when the curtain came down and the student actors took their final bow. Any moment now, she could duck out.

But when the audience finished clapping, Mr. Dobson headed to the stage.

After complimenting the students' efforts, the principal cleared his throat. "I'd like to make some final remarks, if I may. It's been a wonderful year for Pershing School. Our fund-raiser was a huge success, and we are constructing a new school gym." Mr. Dobson paused at the round of applause and cheers. "Great thanks go to Cole Serenghetti and his company for donating construction services. I'm also extremely pleased to announce the new gym will be called The Serg Serenghetti Athletic Building."

Marisa's gaze shot to Cole, but he was looking at Mr. Dobson, clapping like everyone else.

No one got a campus building named after them without making a major monetary donation. In all likelihood, Cole had made a significant cash pledge in addition to donating construction services.

But why?

She'd worked so hard to overcome his resistance to helping with Pershing Shines Bright. The only reason he'd agreed to participate was because of the lucrative construction contract. But now even that profit had evaporated because Cole was making a hefty donation to the school.

Mr. Dobson waited for the audience to settle down. "I'd also like to take this opportunity to welcome our new assistant principal starting next year, Ms. Marisa Danieli."

Marisa blinked, shocked. She hadn't expected that announcement tonight. Caught by surprise, she felt flustered, her heart beginning to pound. Most of all, she felt Cole's eyes on her.

"Ms. Danieli earned her undergraduate and master's degrees from the University of Massachusetts at Amherst. She has been a beloved teacher at Pershing for almost ten years, and a tireless and invaluable member of the school community. Marisa, please come up here, and everyone, join me in congratulating her."

Marisa felt a squeeze on her arm as one of her fellow teachers congratulated her, and then she got up and walked to the stage on rubbery legs. The audience applauded, and there were hoots and hollers from the student body.

The minute Marisa was on stage, she sought out Cole with her eyes, but he was inscrutable, clapping along with everyone else. Had he played a role in her promotion? Had he put in a good word for her, as the school's current and likely most valuable benefactor?

She felt the prickle of tears.

Mr. Dobson was looking at her expectantly, so she cleared her throat and forced herself to speak. "Thank you. I'm thrilled to be Pershing School's new assistant principal. Almost twenty years ago, I walked through the front doors here for the first time. I was a scholarship student, and Pershing changed my life." She paused. "You could say I've gone from being called to the principal's office to having the room next to the principal's office. The distance is short, but the road's been long!"

There was a smattering of laughter and a lot of applause.

"I'm looking forward to my new role." Marisa smiled and then shook hands with Mr. Dobson.

As she stepped off the stage and made her way back to her seat, the principal wished everyone a good night, and the audience began to stand and gather their things.

Marisa hoped she could make a quick escape. She needed to get her emotions under control and to take time to process everything that had happened. But she was waylaid by congratulations, and by the time she was finished, Cole stood at the end of her aisle.

Cole's expression gave nothing away. She, on the other hand, was crumbling.

She pasted a smile on her face and took the initiative—she was the new assistant principal, after all. "Congratulations. You must be thrilled about the new building being named for your father."

"He's excited about the honor."

They stared at each other.

She clasped her hands together to keep from fidgeting. It was either that or give in to the urge to touch him. "So you're ready to embrace your alma mater?"

"That's one way to interpret a large donation."

"Thank you."

Cole still looked indecipherable. "Are you speaking in your role as the new assistant principal?"

"Yes." *And as the woman who loves you.*

He nodded curtly.

"Did you put in a good word for me?" she asked impulsively, knowing she might not get another chance. "Did you pull strings?"

"Does it matter?"

"Did you?" she persisted against all reason.

Cole shrugged. "It turns out my endorsement wasn't needed. You were the overwhelming favorite for the job."

She swallowed. "Thank you."

"You worked hard. You got what you wanted."

Not quite. She didn't have him. She'd never have him.

Just then, a Pershing board member came up to them. "Cole, there's someone I'd like to introduce you to."

Marisa was thankful to be saved from any additional awkwardness with Cole. Murmuring her goodbyes, she turned and fled down the aisle, head bent. She was sure anyone who saw her face would be able to read the raw emotion on it.

Tears welled again, and she made for the exit nearest the stage. Everyone else was streaming toward the doors at the back of the auditorium, which led to the street and parking lot. But she needed a moment alone before reaching her car. She didn't know if she could manage even a small blithe lie to explain away why she was crying.

In the hall beyond the exit, she made a beeline for the closest door, and found herself in the theater department's dimly lit prop room. Furniture was stacked everywhere, some of it covered by drop cloths.

Hearing footsteps outside, she reached behind her and turned the lock on the door and then leaned against the frame.

Someone tried the knob. "Marisa?"

Cole. She said nothing—hoping he'd go away.

"Marisa?" Cole knocked. "Are you okay?"

No, she wasn't. He didn't love her. He was leaving. Nothing was okay.

"You looked upset when you said goodbye. Let me in, sweet pea."

Why? So he could leave her again? She didn't think she could stand it. She strangled a sob and hoped he didn't hear it.

She heard Cole move away from the door, and irrational disappointment hit. Moments later, however, she heard the click of a lock, and then the door was creaking open.

She stepped back and turned to face Cole. "Underhanded and sneaky."

He pocketed a Swiss Army knife. "I learned to pick locks in the Boy Scouts." Then he looked around the room. "We have to stop meeting this way."

"We're safe. The sofa is still onstage."

Cole searched her face and then quirked his lips. "Depends on how you define safe."

Marisa's heart clenched. No, she wasn't safe…and yet she felt like she was home whenever she was near him. "Is there anything you do that doesn't involve bulldozing?"

"Not if I'm going to continue to be the CEO of Serenghetti Construction."

Her eyes went wide. "Is that what you want?"

He gazed at her and then slowly stepped forward, his look tender. He lifted her chin and brushed a thumb across her cheek. "I want you. Marisa, I love you."

She parted her lips and sucked in a tremulous breath, her world tilting.

"I've never said those words to a woman before." He glanced around the storage room before his gaze came back to hers. "And this isn't the way I was envisioning things, but the word at the Puck & Shoot is that you told Sal you wouldn't take him back. Give me a chance, sweet pea."

"You're leaving," she said in a wobbly voice.

"No, I'm not. I'm not taking the job in Wisconsin. I'm staying here to run Serenghetti Construction."

She rested her hand on his arm. "You were angry at me in high school because I interfered with your hockey dreams. I'm not going to make the same mistake twice."

"You're not," he said affectionately. "I'll be coaching here in Welsdale. I'll be teaching teenagers who want to improve their game for a shot at a college scholarship or even the NHL." He paused. "Because I know how life-changing those college scholarships can be."

Her heart swelled. She adored this man.

"The more time I had to think about selling Serenghetti Construction, the more it didn't seem right. I had to acknowledge that construction is in my blood." He tilted his head. "Besides, I've got some ideas, including growing the business into a real estate development firm."

Marisa smiled. "Face it, Serenghetti Construction is

just another arena for you to be competitive. That's why you were so set on winning over JM Construction. And who knows? The kids you're coaching may give you another chance at a hockey championship."

"Sometimes, Marisa, I swear you know me better than I know myself." He brushed her lips with his.

"Hang on to that thought because I plan to be around a lot." Cole was good, strong and hardworking. He also happened to be able to make her feel like the sexiest woman alive. He was the person she'd always been looking for.

"You're marrying a construction guy."

"Are you proposing?"

He twined his fingers with hers and raised her hand to his lips. "Damn right."

"I'm ratting you out, Cole, and this time I don't care who finds out." Her voice grew husky with emotion. "I'm telling everyone that you confessed your undying love for me. That you proposed!"

He kissed her. "You forgot *he can't keep his hands off me*, *he talks dirty to me*, and *he gets hard just thinking about me*."

"That's right."

"I'm in love with you."

"Good to know. I love you, too."

She sighed, and he kissed her again.

Epilogue

If they pulled this off, it would be Cole's biggest prank ever.

Leave it to her soon-to-be husband to involve her in the ultimate practical joke. Around her, guests mingled while waitstaff circulated with hors d'oeuvres. Everyone was unaware of what was to come next.

Marisa rubbed nervous palms on her column dress and then brushed aside the curls of hair that caressed her naked shoulders. As she did so, the diamond ring on her finger caught and reflected the light of the chandelier in the main ballroom of the Welsdale Golf & Tennis Club.

At the dais, Cole cleared his throat and called for attention, wineglass in hand. When everyone quieted, he said, "Thank you for joining us tonight. Marisa and I wanted to throw a big party to celebrate our engagement, so there are over two hundred of you here. Big love, big party—"

There was a smattering of laughter and applause.

Cole straightened his tie. "As some of you know, Marisa and I have had more excitement on the way to the altar than most people witness in an NHL game."

Their guests grinned and laughed.

"I had a crush on her in high school." He paused. "And I know what you all are thinking. Pershing's super jock and practical joker thought he had a chance with the beautiful, smart girl who sat in front of him in economics class? She had a mind and a body that turned him into brainless teenage mush."

Marisa swallowed against the sudden lump in her throat.

Cole shrugged. "So I did the only logical thing. I hid how I felt and told no one. Flash forward fifteen years. I got lucky when my fantasy woman skated onto my rink again. This time I knew I wasn't going to let her get away. I asked her to marry me."

Marisa blinked rapidly. Everything Cole had said was true, and yet, he'd cast it in a light that she'd never seen before.

Cole extended his arm. "Marisa, I love you."

A path opened for Marisa as people stepped aside. On shaky legs, she walked toward Cole, who gazed at her with love in his eyes. She placed her hand in his, and raising the skirt of her dress with the other she stepped up onto the dais.

Their friends and family hooted and clapped.

"That was quite a speech," she murmured for Cole's ears only. "I nearly ruined my makeup."

He grinned. "You would have looked gorgeous for the photos anyway."

"You're blinded by love."

"I wouldn't have it any other way, sweet pea." He gave her a quick peck on the lips before turning back to their audience, keeping his hand linked with hers.

"Save the PDA for the honeymoon," Jordan called from the side of the room, to much laughter.

"Thanks for the great lead-in," Cole answered. "Because Marisa and I are getting married. Tonight. Right now."

There were audible gasps, and people looked at each other.

The officiant she and Cole had chosen stepped forward from the side of the room.

"Surprise," Cole announced, and then he pulled Marisa into his embrace for another kiss.

When Cole had first suggested the idea of a surprise wedding, Marisa had thought he was kidding, but she couldn't have asked for anything more. She felt like a bride in every sense. She'd paired an embroidered lace-and-ivory gown with high-heeled gold sandals. And of course, she'd marry Cole anytime, anywhere.

There was a flurry of activity as their guests allowed themselves to be shepherded out of the ballroom and into one that had been secretly set up for a wedding ceremony. A photographer would be documenting the festivities, and a florist waited nearby to hand Marisa a tightly packed bouquet of white roses.

Marisa felt her heart swell, and then caught Cole's grin. Suddenly struck with an idea, she bit back a mischievous smile.

"Oh, Cole, this has been so overwhelming. I think…

I think…" She closed her eyes and pretended to swoon melodramatically.

Cole wrapped strong arms around her. "Marisa?"

She opened her eyes and said teasingly, "I'll be falling into your embrace for the rest of our lives."

Cole grinned. "I'll always be here to catch you."

And they sealed their bargain with a kiss.

* * * * *

*If you liked this novel, pick up these other
sexy reads from Anna DePalo*

*HAVING THE TYCOON'S BABY
UNDER THE TYCOON'S PROTECTION
TYCOON TAKES REVENGE
CAPTIVATED BY THE TYCOON
AN IMPROPER AFFAIR
CEO'S MARRIAGE SEDUCTION
HIS BLACK SHEEP BRIDE
ONE NIGHT WITH PRINCE CHARMING
IMPROPERLY WED*

All available now from Harlequin Desire!

***

*If you're on Twitter, tell us what you think of
Harlequin Desire! #harlequindesire*

SPECIAL EXCERPT FROM

HARLEQUIN® *Desire*

Navy SEAL Gavin Blake has returned home to the ranch he loves to make sure beautiful Layla Harris leaves his family's spread...

Read on for a sneak peek at
THE RANCHER RETURNS,
by New York Times *bestselling author*
Brenda Jackson,
the first in **THE WESTMORELAND LEGACY** series!

Gavin grabbed his duffel from the truck. He tilted his Stetson back on his head and looked at the car parked in front of his grandmother's guest cottage. Gavin hoped his grandmother hadn't extended an invitation for that professor to stay on their property as well as dig on their land. He didn't want anyone taking advantage of his family.

He'd taken one step onto the porch when the front door swung open and his grandmother walked out. She was smiling, and when she opened her arms, he dropped his duffel bag and walked straight into the hug awaiting him.

"Welcome home, Gavin," she said. "I didn't expect you for a few months yet. Did everything go okay?"

He smiled. She always asked him the same thing, knowing full well that because of the classified nature of his job as a SEAL, he couldn't tell her anything. "Yes, Gramma Mel, everything went okay. I'm back because—"

He blinked, not sure he was seeing straight. A woman stood in the doorway, but she wasn't just *some* woman. She had to be the most gorgeous woman he'd ever seen. Hell, she looked like everything he'd ever fantasized a woman to be, even while fully clothed in jeans and a pullover sweater.

Gavin studied her features, trying to figure out what had him spellbound. Was it the caramel-colored skin, dark chocolate eyes, dimpled cheeks, button nose or well-defined, kissable lips? Maybe every single thing.

Not waiting for his grandmother to make introductions, his mouth eased into a smile. He reached out his hand and said, "Hello, I'm Gavin."

The moment their hands touched, a jolt of desire shot through his body. Nothing like this had ever happened to him before. From the expression that flashed in her eyes, he knew she felt it, as well.

"It's nice meeting you, Gavin," she said softly. "Layla Harris."

Harris? His aroused senses suddenly screeched to a stop. Did she say *Harris*? Was Layla related to this Professor Harris? Was she part of the excavation team?

Now he had even more questions, and he was determined to get some answers.

Don't miss
THE RANCHER RETURNS
by New York Times *bestselling author Brenda Jackson,
available October 2016 wherever
Harlequin® Desire books and ebooks are sold.*

www.Harlequin.com

Whatever You're Into… Passionate Reads

Looking for more passionate reads from Harlequin®?
Fear not! Harlequin® Presents, Harlequin® Desire and
Harlequin® Blaze offer you irresistible romance stories
featuring powerful heroes.

◆HARLEQUIN *Presents*.

Do you want alpha males, decadent glamour and jet-set
lifestyles? Step into the sensational, sophisticated world of
Harlequin® Presents, where sinfully tempting heroes ignite a
fierce and wickedly irresistible passion!

◆HARLEQUIN *Desire*

Harlequin® Desire novels are powerful, passionate and
provocative contemporary romances set against a backdrop of
wealth, privilege and sweeping family saga. Alpha heroes with
a soft side meet strong-willed but vulnerable heroines amid a
dramatic world of divided loyalties, high-stakes conflict and
intense emotion.

◆HARLEQUIN *Blaze*

Harlequin® Blaze stories sizzle with strong heroines and
irresistible heroes playing the game of modern love and lust.
They're fun, sexy and always steamy.

Be sure to check out our full selection of books
within each series every month!

www.Harlequin.com